About the Author.

David was born and raised in Scotland but has spent most of his years overseas, working in bars, advertising and anything else that paid a wage. Café Dawn is his second novel. The first, The Ghost of Bobby, a young teen ghost story is also available on Amazon and is currently used in a Glasgow secondary school as critical reading for first year students.
Café Dawn was conceived after a conversation one day with his daughter Jade. And then another with an old friend. Two thoughts merged and became Café Dawn.

Copyright

Cafe Dawn

© *2021, D. Limond Miller*

Self-published

All rights reserved.

No part of this publication may be reproduced, stored in a retrieval system, stored in a database and / or published in any form or by any means, electronic, mechanical, photocopying, recording or otherwise, without the prior written permission of the publisher.

Café Dawn.
August 1970 - October 1980.

For Jade. Always.

Chapter 1.

The first dream that Walter Mack remembered as a boy was one that became a recurring ordeal throughout his childhood, and one he recalled and dreamt regularly throughout his early adulthood.

On becoming a young man of twenty, at best he was of average height and build, with dark brown hair that matched large, dark brown eyes. There was a quiet steeliness in his demeanour that not everyone detected, and he often over-reacted to threats of any sort, to the serious detriment of those who'd picked on or underestimated him.

Walter had compassion for those who were weak and bruised- he worried about them too much- just as he had a disproportionate amount of disdain for the uncaring and arrogant.

In his recurring dream, he was perhaps five years old, sitting behind his mother on a motorbike. His father was also on a motorbike, but in front of them, the headlights of his bike picked out a never-ending empty, sandy road as they drove through a dark night. On either side of them was desert. The motor bikes came to an abrupt stop and Walter's mother pushed him off the bike and onto the road where he landed badly, hurting his elbow. He started to cry. His mother ignored him and drove off behind his father. Walter wailed at them, begging them not to leave him behind. But they kept going and never came back. They didn't even look back.

Walter Mack was alone in the world.

Chapter 2. Brighton, England. August 1970.

Walter stopped in front of the army recruitment centre on Queen's Road in Brighton. At 20 years of age; hungry, homeless and cold, the army recruitment poster in the shop front window looked appealing. A crowd of young lads with face paint, guns, and uniforms seemingly having something pretty tasty to eat as they sat around a campfire in the wild. Home for Walter was one alcoholic parent in a dirty and cold flat in Edinburgh. If she wasn't drunk, she was asleep. Somewhat ironically, his father had been killed in a motorbike accident the year before, 1969. Walter left school when he was fifteen, which required him to ask the headmaster to sign a form he'd been given by a college he had no intention of going to. This was in order to be released from school before he was sixteen. When Walter approached the headmaster, he asked who Walter was. It was a sure sign that he'd made the right decision.

"Come in, come in," the middle- aged man in army dress said to Walter, after he was already inside. "Interested in joining the army?"
Walter said he was, but he didn't really know much about the army and wanted to know what he might do in it. He asked the sergeant what he might be qualified to do. Walter had got into the habit of explaining upfront to potential employers that he had no qualifications of any level at all, and he knew that this excluded him from most lines of work. Saying this upfront saved time.

Walter looked at the stripes on the man's arm as he extended it for a strong army handshake; he seemed like an honest man.

After a good twenty minutes going through various opportunities that might be open to Walter, the Marine Corps was the one that appealed most to him. The physical exertion and the travel appealed, but so did the idea of camaraderie, and being part of something. He'd be part of the Royal Marines, a world- famous group of people. Food, security, money. And all the marines wanted in return was him. He would have to commit to three years at a minimum but if that was all, then there was nothing to think about.

At that point in time, he had no plans for the rest of his life. The only thing that niggled a little in the back of his mind was that he wasn't sure what skills he'd pick up beyond battle skills: perhaps a knowledge of weapons and survival skills? To a young man like Walter, with no one, and nothing except a fluctuating will to live, and the pursuit of happiness on a good day; overall, it felt like a pretty good trade off. Wise beyond his years, he knew that at the very least, time in the marines would keep him fed and give him time to think.

Like many of Walter's decisions made in the early years, this was done on the spot. It was madness- he still knew close to nothing about the Royal Marines- and yet it would turn out to be an inspired decision, and life changing for him in both good ways, and bad. It was all part of the making of Walter Mack.

Chapter 3. Dartmoor.

A week after signing up, Walter was on a train to Lympstone near Exeter, where all those wishing to join the marines underwent a variety of tests in order to be admitted. He hadn't officially been admitted yet. The selection process was challenging, regarded as the toughest of all NATO members' training programmes. While there was a written element to the training, it was the thirty- two weeks of physical hell that made it tough to qualify for admission. Still, Walter arrived keen to get going.

His first night in the barracks was no different to every other first night in those barracks that had gone before him. Someone wanted to be top dog. There was always someone like that. The majority of recruits only wanted to be part of the training and succeed: some of them were always going to be weaker and more fearful than the rest. Bullies could smell them out.

Given his emaciated appearance, weighing around thirsty pounds less than the average recruit in the room, and with feeble biceps which were noticeable when he stripped to the waist, everyone assumed that Walter was the weakest of all.

The bullying started with verbal poking and came from a large, ugly young man named Smythe. He had an accent that Walter recognised as Leeds, perhaps, or possibly Mancunian. He wasn't sure, but north of England somewhere. Smythe was pockmarked, white as a sheet and already losing his blond, greasy hair. Physically, he wasn't tall- probably just average height- but he was built like an ox.

Smythe walked from bunk to bunk talking to people, sizing them up as everyone tried to chill on the first evening by unpacking, smoking, talking in small groups, playing cards. Walter was on his own, lying on his back reading a book titled, "The History of the Royal Marines" with his pillows doubled over to support his neck, a cigarette in his mouth and his feet crossed at the ankles.

"My sister's got bigger muscles than you, mate." Smythe looked round the room to see who was watching and listening. It had started, so everyone turned to look. Some were excited at the prospect of the upcoming scene, others saddened by it, and some just glad they weren't the focus of Smythe's attention.

Walter looked up at Smythe but said nothing. He started reading again.
He could see what was coming a mile off. True to form, Smythe leaned over and with one hand, swept Walter's feet off the bed causing him to sit up. Walter stood, taking a hammer that lay prepared under the top cover of his bed and moved forward fast as a whippet, taking Smythe by surprise. He hit him on the shoulder with extreme force, sending Smythe to his knees, howling. Walter didn't bother saying anything to him or to anyone else. There was no need to.

No one confronted Walter again. Smythe was able to continue through the course, albeit in constant pain but he didn't think about reporting Walter; he'd be laughed out of the room.

Towards the end of week thirty – two, his final week's training- the commando tests- Walter chose to apply to combat intelligence as his specialisation, intrigued by the idea of working out what any given enemy or threat to the nation was thinking and was likely to do next, then creating strategies to annul the danger. It was like chess. Combat intelligence was the one part of The History of the Royal Marines that he had read over and over. It piqued his curiosity. He had lots of questions to ask his interviewer, Colonel McLellan, the next day.

Chapter 4. The Road to Morocco.

"Do you always keep a hammer under your bed cover?" asked the Colonel.
Walter was in a room facing five people, none of whom had introduced themselves except for Colonel McLellan.

"I do," said Walter.

"And why might that be?" asked McLellan.

"Well, for as long as I can remember- and I mean, as long as I can remember- from time to time, there has been someone hovering around my bed that I don't want hovering around because they have ill intent. And so, I learned that the best way to sleep peacefully and to get rid of any threat is to keep a hammer close by. I'm just being honest with you, so if that means you're not interested in me, just say so now, and I'll apply to do something else."

The five interviewers looked into Walter's eyes, each processing the brutal honesty of his words, trying to work out exactly what that statement said about the young man standing defiantly in front of them.

"I should let you know that there won't be any charges following your assault on Smythe. He's an arse," McLellan said.

"To be clear," said one of the four nameless men, "we could bring charges, and could have brought them when the incident happened, but your actions interested us. No fuss, no follow up. No drama. Clinical. My name is Clarke. We're all from combat intelligence. Each of us has a different role in the division, but we're all interested in recruiting the right people as the role of combat intelligence in the army expands."

"How do you know that I assaulted Smythe?" asked Walter.

"Well, let's call that 'combat intelligence', shall we?" answered McLellan.

Walter smiled. He liked these guys.

Over the course of the hours of interviewing that followed, Walter surprised himself by openly answering questions about his life: his isolated childhood, his resulting loneliness and lack of trust in anyone other than himself; his lack of education, his lack of friends and his lack of trust in authority. He couldn't imagine that they'd want to recruit him after all he revealed. It had been hours of talking about everything he lacked. But as bright as Walter was, he was still young, and didn't realise that what he saw as failure in himself, those people asking the questions saw things that interested them, not failure. Among them were survival instincts, and perseverance. For all of Walter's lack of education, he was clearly well read, intelligent, and articulate. His irreverence and relaxed manner indicated surface confidence; his attachment to his hammer indicated abandonment, aggression and survival, but not fear.

"Do you trust anyone?" asked McLellan.

"No." replied Walter.

"You'd need to trust people in the teams you work with, were you to be asked to join us."

"Every single person I've ever wanted to trust has let me down." said Walter. "I can't just say I'm going to trust people because they tell me to trust them. But I can give them the benefit of the doubt."

The five interviewers exchanged glances, then McLellan welcomed Walter to combat intelligence. This young man had potential, but a lot of rough edges to smooth out, he thought. They'd need to earn his trust. It was usually the other way round.

The next morning at 5am, Walter, dressed in civilian clothes, boarded a military plane along with numerous people he'd never seen before, on route to Marrakech. It was the start of a journey for Walter in which he'd find hate and money, good food, love, and eventually, peace. Each decision he made, influenced by the previous one, would determine his future.

Chapter 5. Marrakech, 1971.

Walter lived on a military base, which wasn't officially a military base but instead posed as an Anglo-French trade mission. It was a group of interlinked low rise, dull and scruffy buildings in the business heart of Marrakech; Gueliz, where a number of European businesses and residential communities were based. It was a monumentally boring place. In his time off, Walter would head out to the tourist district of Jemma el-Fnaa, where he was interested in soaking up the atmosphere of the markets and bars. He loved the food stalls, and spent hours walking through them, imbibing the powerful smell of spices that hung in the air. He took to smoking kif in one or two of the cafés and he loved the change in his state of being that it induced. For Walter, this unusual lifestyle was closer to a home life than anything he'd felt before.

Despite the reservations he'd stated during his interview, over time he came to like the company of some of his colleagues, both British and French, and he gained a feeling of camaraderie which he'd never felt before. It was camaraderie at a distance in his case. He enjoyed going out at night with the French guys more than the British ones because he didn't speak a word of French, so he could enjoy the company without engaging in conversation. He'd smile when they laughed, drink when they drank and smoked when they did. It worked perfectly for him. They never asked anything of him, and never questioned his presence because they knew he couldn't understand anything they said. And they wouldn't speak English when out drinking, just for his sake. All in all, they were good guys.

Daytimes involved intense training, including learning about the Arab world, political and terrorist threats to Europe and the Arab world. Everybody seemed to want to kill everybody else. It interested Walter intensely, and the more he understood, the more he learned about the need to listen and weigh things up before making judgements. Hasty decisions seemed to lead to problems. Through a combination of Arab civilians, military intelligence shared among the western nations (and hidden from each other in equal measure) and through threats and bribery to anyone who had useful information, Walter began to work out how combat intelligence worked- it was pretty much how the world worked. He no longer felt the need to sleep with a hammer in his bed. He lived in a world where lies were spread, people disappeared, arms were bought and sold, religions clashed, and war always seemed to be on the horizon. Oddly, he felt comfortable in it but that was because he had an element of stability in his private life.

Even as he enjoyed his role, the security, the regular food and the regimen, he knew that this was no route to a happy life for him. It was temporary because somehow, he needed to find peace of mind; he just didn't know how.

Since childhood, he had never slept soundly through the night. Either the recurring dream or a sense of unease would wake him at some point. He wondered if he'd ever get a full night's sleep.

Each day at work he would gather information on bad people and their planned actions, and he'd help map out a strategy to combat it. The longer he carried out his important role in the name of his country's security – which it was – (albeit a small role) the more he could smell the scent of hate in his clothes when he dressed in the mornings. For it was hate that seemed to be driving everything around him and it manifested itself in the air he breathed. He understood that he helped save lives in northern Africa, and overseas too, but it seemed that there was a limit to how long he or anyone could carry on living in this world. He knew the army had been good to him since the day he joined but one day he'd need to find a way out. There wasn't an immediate rush, however, because the heat and the distance from his old home life still enveloped him every day like a warm blanket. Anything was better than the cold, damp and dark.

Every month or so he and others would be put on a military plane in the early hours and flown south east for several days. Walter would see the sun rise as they flew and be in wonder at the sight of the changing landscape below him. The bland desert terrain was beautiful to him, and while everyone else complained of the heat, he loved it. Whenever he began to un-love it, he'd think of the cold and damp house he'd grown up in, and he'd immediately love the heat again.

The desert training was where Walter and hundreds of others from various units related to the French, American and British military trained in many different skills. He learned about explosives and survival skills. When it came to unarmed combat, Walter did well, but had to work harder than others due to being a little smaller and lighter than others. He did not lack courage though, so he survived and prospered over time, while suffering broken teeth and bones. The better he became, the fewer injuries he sustained. After four years, he had skills that every hooligan on the streets of Britain would have paid any amount of money for.

Where Walter excelled markedly beyond everyone else in training though, was in armed combat. He excelled on the sniper range. He was taught about distance, wind factors, bullets, guns, humidity, dry air, light, camouflage, speed, packing and unpacking rifles, concealment, constructing and deconstructing guns. Stage by stage Walter learned, and whenever there was a target competition, he beat everyone, always. He missed absolutely nothing. During sniper exercises his heart rate fell as his breathing slowed, allowing him to focus then squeeze.

He was watched carefully during all exercises, and it was remarked by others how different his unarmed and armed combat styles were. Unarmed, he used speed where he lacked mass. When armed, he took his time, letting the weapon do the work for him.
He was creating a lot of interest within the army. And outside of it too.

Five years into the job in Marrakech it seemed as if everyone he had worked with had come and gone. Each person who'd come in had eventually asked to get out, and in time had been transferred away having completed their tour of duty. Everyone got out except Walter because he had nowhere to go. He stayed put and the army was happy to keep him in Marrakech.

Chapter 6. Marrakech, 1976. Riding a Horse that's been Skinned.

"You've done well; very much as I expected when I first recruited you, Mack. Perhaps even better." said Colonel McLellan.

"Thank you, Sir. It's good to see you. What are you doing out here, may I ask?"

"I've been out a number of times before but never had time to meet with you, or indeed the majority of our people. I tend to keep a low profile and talk only with those I need to talk with." Nothing more was going to be said on the matter, that was obvious.

"And so," McLellan leaned back, appraising Walter as if he was an antique vase "what is next for you, Mack?"

"Honestly Sir, the army has been great for me and I'm grateful that you brought me on to your team but I'm beginning to feel tired of living in this world of combat intelligence. I do understand that we're on the good side; well, I hope we are"- McLellan raised his eyebrows at that – "but going into work feels less rewarding each day because we never seem to progress. I know we do, of course we do, I see the statistics myself, it's just that it's a dark place to live in. I grew up in a dark place and don't want to spend the rest of my life in it."

"How do you feel about the people you've had to kill, Mack?"

"There have been very few, and it's always been part of a well thought out and planned exercise. It's been necessary, is what I'm saying. That's part of what the army does, and I've done it on behalf of a country, trying to do the right thing. Honestly, the people I've had to kill have been truly hideous, and in each case, it's been justified in my mind because it led to saved lives. They were terrorists, all of them. I know that for a fact because I'm the one who will have built up the intelligence on them. I can sleep at night."

The opposite was true of course. Walter still hadn't slept solidly through the night since he was a little boy. He was always at unease, his mind always whirring, the recurring dream perennially surfacing.

"Are you planning to leave the army then?" asked McLellan. "And if so, what are you going to do?"

"That's the thing Sir, I do want to leave, but I don't know where I'd go. I don't want to join a security company or become an insurance salesman. I just don't think I'd enjoy doing anything that most other people seem to do."

"What would you really like to do Mack– if you had a choice?"

"I'd like to wake up in a place where the sun shines most days, learn how to cook and own the best café in the world."

"That's pretty clear. I'd never have expected an answer like that from you in a million years, Mack." McLellan smiled. "How long have you been thinking about learning to cook?"

"For as long as I can remember. Most of my childhood I went hungry, and when I ate, it was disgusting food. My home was cold and damp. Everyone in my life was unfriendly. If I had a café, it would be warm and friendly, with great food. There would be a sign outside the door: 'no assholes.'"

McLellan laughed heartily, then put on his thoughtful face.

"Let me ask you a question, Mack. And I'll talk for a bit before I get to the question, so be patient." He continued without giving Walter a chance to reply.

"From time to time my colleagues and I, and indeed various other branches of what makes up our fine military and government, come across something that falls between the cracks. Now what I mean by that is that a dangerous individual or a group surfaces that doesn't fit the "to be sorted" remit of any of our military, intelligence, or policing services- it falls in between the cracks. No one really wants to deal with it. The problems are usually distasteful affairs, often brought to our, or indeed another country's services by large criminal organisations. These criminal organisations don't do it out of the goodness of their hearts. They do it because it's an opportunity to remove another criminal element which they don't want around. For our part, we look at the situation and weigh up the credence of the threat that has been brought to our attention and the motives of the group that has brought the problem to our attention. An example might be one criminal organisation knowing that one of its rivals– who they'd like to be rid of– have got their hands on stolen military weaponry which they will likely sell on to the highest bidder, no matter how heinous a buyer that might be: that kind of thing. Clear?" McLellan asked. Walter nodded and McLellan continued.

"So, having appraised such a situation we decide whether we should act or not; knowing that if we do, it's usually to the advantage of the criminal outfit that has brought it to our attention. Often, it's like being asked to watch a fight between two Nazis and being asked which one you'd like to win. Our course of action is usually one which no government wants to take responsibility for because it involves work that is technically illegal, and indeed, no one within our security services wants to take responsibility for. Everyone just wants the problem to go away, but of course, it won't. It just gets worse if not acted upon. And so, either we, that's me, or someone in one of our other services deals with it and no questions are ever asked. And the problem vanishes overnight."

McLellan took a deep breath, then paused.

"I have a proposal for you Mack- something which may appeal to you, or let me put it another way, something that may work for you given the situation you are in, your various skill sets taught to you by the army, and what you want your future to look like. But importantly, Mack, I think it may work for you given the misery of your formative years. Would you like to hear what I have in mind?"

Walter had bristled at the mention of his childhood because it felt like a low blow. McLellan was fully aware of Walter's past. Still, Walter didn't like to talk about it. That said, he'd only just mentioned it to McLellan himself, so he said nothing, and instead just nodded his agreement.

McLellan spent exactly one hour providing Walter with more information on the world of problems that fell between the cracks and how they were resolved. It was precisely people like Walter Mack who ultimately did the dirty work; people who no longer wished to remain in the military. They weren't mercenaries who did it for the money. They were trustworthy and discreet people who did things that others wouldn't do as they exited the army– and as they did so, they'd rid the world of an indisputable menace.

McLellan had paused again to ensure that he was being clear.

The biggest issue, he went on to explain, was that the army couldn't and didn't pay for the work, the criminal element that the army chose to work with paid, and in almost every case, the work involved killing someone. It would be a life changing amount of money, but the real upside was that the individual being targeted would be someone who was "army checked guilty", without question, of causing harm and grief to untold numbers of innocents.

That said, it is walking a moral tightrope McLellan told him.

It was true. Walter was uneasy. He felt as if he was being asked to ride a horse that had been skinned. Nothing but trouble would lie ahead, if things weren't managed very carefully.

"I know what you're thinking Mack, and you're right. It is ugly, morally questionable, and illegal. But you've seen enough of how the world works in real life."

Walter had already seen more than his fair share.

"Could I accept and then pull out later?" he asked.

"You could, but the problem is, once you make an agreement with illegal entities, and they've exposed themselves to you it's not wise to let them down. They're not a forgiving bunch."

As Walter sat back and pondered, McLellan continued to talk, telling him about the two feuding parties he was thinking of, one based there in Morocco, the other in Zurich. The grievances between them seemed to be boiling up. One entity was run by a very corrupt but usually non-violent owner based in Marrakech who ran a vast number of nightclubs and bars, some in Morocco but mostly across southern Spain. He made a great deal of money from them, as well as a considerable amount of money from laundering his and other people's money. The other entity, the one that would be Walter's target, trafficked children on an unprecedented scale both in terms of numbers and the degree of violence with which it was carried out. He kept various authorities in different places at bay through intimidation, through legal jurisdiction grey areas and bribery, all done from his home in Zurich where he also ran a small private bank. He wasn't Moroccan, he was Swiss. He was also trying to expand his business enterprises to nightclubs and bars in Spain's coastal resorts therefore treading on the toes of the other entity who had been in touch with McLellan.

"How much is enough?" asked Walter thinking that surely running a private Swiss bank would pay an eye watering amount of money.

McLellan nodded, understanding what Walter meant.

"It's not about the money– he was born rich. He enjoys what he does, trafficking children. He bathes in misery. It's an addiction. He's a vile character. Married with children but leading a promiscuous and dark sexual life."

McLellan paused again, just talking of this man was tiring.

Walter shifted in his chair waiting for McLellan to continue, impressed by him. He'd done his homework well. Walter's sad, lonely and frightened childhood, coupled with experiences which led him to keep a hammer in bed with him meant that his feeling towards child traffickers was nothing short of revulsion and hatred. McLellan had systems and processes in place so that people in his team, like the increasingly unhappy Walter, would be identified early and monitored, then approached if needed. Recent reports suggested that the writing was on the wall with Walter and all McLellan had to do was leave him in Morocco until the time would come to speak with him, which was now.

"Remember this, Mack. While you'd get paid by criminals, and we'd keep our distance from you– you'd resign from the army- you'd be doing the job for me– for us. And if you ever need to come to me at some point in the future, you will have a way to reach us. I will be in the army for a long time to come. Even when I'm gone you won't be forgotten. That said, you can choose never to contact us afterwards knowing that we'll never come to you to ask to help a second time. These jobs are one offs. A second time would make it mercenary. Once is a service, and a way out."

"But why don't the Moroccan authorities or the Swiss or Spanish ones take care of this?" said Walter, listening to McLellan but jumping to questions.

"Because it's seen as an international problem, not just a problem for one of these three countries. And frankly, we don't trust any of the countries involved to deal with it quickly or properly. We're not even sure that they want to do anything. A lot of people are paid vast sums to look the other way. Nothing about this is a British problem and yet we've ended up having to sort it out. It happens a lot."

It seemed wholly ridiculous to Walter, and yet during his time with combat intelligence he'd witnessed extraordinary amounts of incompetence, evil and uncaring among private citizens, and across governments, police forces and militaries. No wonder the world was in such a mess. What was wrong with people?

As much as Walter struggled with the idea of killing someone for money, a child trafficker was about as justifiable as it'd get. On the other hand, who was he to say it was alright? His views were flip flopping like a fish out of water. Surely the worst that could happen is that he'd be paid, and a child trafficker would be dead? Unless of course it went wrong and he was killed himself..

Despite all the reasons for saying no, Walter recognised that this opportunity, no matter how murky, could be beneficial to him and countless innocents.

"When you say life changing money, how much do you mean?" He felt guilty for asking, but when McLellan told him how much, Walter nearly fell off his chair. He'd never need to work again.

"Why don't you do it yourself, Colonel?"

"I like the army and I like solving these problems that crop up from time to time. It is a good cause, no matter how ugly the means. But who knows, maybe one day I'll want to leave the army, just like you – and maybe there'll be someone equally repulsive that I can rid the world of in exchange for the freedom to do as I please for the rest of my days. Because that's what this one last squeeze of a trigger can do for you, Mack. Absolute freedom. Take five minutes to read our file on Weber, the man in question."

McLellan handed a manila file to Walter who took it and removed the document about Weber that lay inside. It took him five minutes to read it, just as McLellan had said. Afterwards, he felt sick.

"Are you in or out?" McLellan asked him.

"Can you not find someone else to get rid of this man?"

"Of course, I could easily find someone to get rid of him. But not necessarily someone I trust to do things properly, or someone who won't turn this kind of thing into a vocation, or won't keep quiet about it until the end of their days. This isn't about death, Mack, this is about life and trust. How many people do you trust?"

Chapter 7. The Spice Market, Marrakech,1976.

The early evening sun touched Walter's shoulders as he stood at the corner of the market admiring the mass of stalls and the masses of men and women who bustled about buying and selling what was on offer. From where he stood, he could smell donkey shit, or camel shit– he wasn't sure which– but knew that it'd disappear as he made his way through the market and passed the spice stalls where the cornerstone spices of Moroccan cooking; ginger, black pepper, turmeric and cumin were sold.

He wandered lazily on, moving into the market, shifting past interesting and beautiful people of all shapes and sizes, and as he did so, he recognised the powerful scent of cinnamon which vanished as quickly as it had appeared. These walks through the market always made him hungry because he'd grown to love Moroccan food. Wherever he ended up in the world in the future, he'd always eat it.

When on his own time, he'd regularly pass through the market and then into the square on his way to smoke kif, enjoying the warmth of the setting sun in the same way other people enjoyed the warmth from a cat resting on their shoulders while they lounged in a comfortable chair reading a book. It was soothing. He closed his eyes and turned his face to the sky, soaking up the life around him and the good things the sun had to offer. When it dropped out of sight, Walter would walk to 'Hape', a café, for a drink and a smoke. It was quiet and being a regular there, he would be led through to the back where he was allowed to smoke kif. He'd been doing the same thing for five years now. Things had worked perfectly well for both him and the army until recently when Walter had become restless and the ever insightful McLellan had turned up.

This beautiful evening, as the sky turned from light blue to red then to deep blue, he licked his lips as he watched his beer arrive in a frosted glass. It was just what a thirsty young man needed.

The tray with his glass was held by a waiter that Walter hadn't seen before. The man was old, perhaps seventy years Walter guessed, with very dark skin and white whiskers on his skinny face.

"I have a friend who wishes to speak with you. He is in the army, like you- just not the same one."

"Who and where is he?"

"Come."

With the hackles raised on his neck Walter followed the waiter, who still had Walter's beer on the tray, to an alcove at the other side of the bar where a man who looked European sat. The waiter placed Walter's beer on the table and walked off. The European looking man motioned to Walter to sit. He looked like the military type but had an easy way about him and didn't seem threatening.

"Why did you need to send the waiter over?" Walter asked. "Why not just walk over yourself and ask me to join you?"

"Well, it's a good indication if you're curious or not."

"Fair enough" said Walter, unimpressed by the needless drama. "Let me just drink some of this beer before it warms."

Walter sipped at his beer, eying the man. He was considerably older than Walter, possibly in his forties. Yes, he was definitely out of the forces he thought, but officer material. He must have come from money too, because, like all people who have grown up surrounded by money, it showed. Wealthy people look healthy. His hair was thick and grey, well-groomed and it fell in front of his face in places, giving him a rakish appearance. He wore an expensive white cotton shirt rolled up at the sleeves and had sunglasses folded and placed in his shirt pocket. He was suave. Walter imagined women would find him attractive, or indeed, some men might too, which led Walter to ask, "What can I do for you?"

"My name is Guy, and I used to work in the French military. I retired around five years ago, and nowadays I'm a consultant. People come to me with problems, and I help solve them. All sorts of problems, all sorts of people. I've heard a number of good things about you from my friends in the army here, and I think I may have some work for you if you're interested." The man paused, and when Walter said nothing, he continued.

"I have a client, a Moroccan man, who would like to meet you. If he's happy with you, then our talks can go a little further. I think you'll like my client. I had heard from another source that you were expecting this meeting to take place?"

"Yes, I was."

"If you do this job correctly- if you're offered this job- you'd be working completely on your own. You'd be paid upfront, with the money put into an account …"

"Stop." said Walter. "I know nothing about such things. I've got a savings account with the Nationwide Building Society in Brighton and a savings account here in Marrakech with the Banque Popular du Maroc which only has some beer money in it. I do not have a secret account in The Caymans under a different name. I have one passport, no secret identity …"

"You stop." said Guy. "Every problem has a solution. You're getting ahead of yourself. You haven't even been offered the work. Today I was just saying hello and confirming a conversation is possible: I will relay to the man I represent that it is indeed possible. Meet me here, same time next week. Do not tell anyone. If you do, we will find out and we will take things no further. Discretion is vital. You work in the army; you know how things are."

With that said, Guy walked off.

Walter ordered another beer then sipped at it, thinking. It was hard for him. He understood right from wrong, but he'd spent his childhood cold, hungry and alone, and his teen years hungry and cold, aggressively defending himself against the violent acts of others. The idea of killing someone no matter how outrageously unpleasant for money didn't sit comfortably with him. He finished his beer, paid for it and decided to skip the kif and head straight back to his room. He wanted to go to the admin duty log to ensure he was off duty at the same time next week. He was still planning to meet Guy.

Chapter 8. Prudence, Marrakech,1976.

Walter wondered what he'd let himself in for as he sat inside a chauffeur driven car waiting for enormous golden gates to open in front of a large, detached house. It was a mansion in fact, not a house. He could see a long driveway behind the gates which led up to a grand three storied white building with a red tiled roof- and on the first floor, a terrace that stretched the entire width of the house. Guy was beside him in the car, very much in facilitator mode now, not answering any questions, simply saying that Walter was safe, there were no commitments, and all would be explained by his client, who was still unnamed.

The gates shuddered when they opened, as if freezing cold, and Walter felt the car move forward at a snail's pace up the driveway past cacti and shrubs on either side. The entrance to the house was framed in magnificent bougainvillea which Walter loved, and he gazed at the opulence of the building. He followed the driver and Guy into the house, past the housekeeper dressed in formal attire who had opened the door, and into a grand reception room. The driver motioned for Walter to sit and wait. Almost immediately after he'd taken a seat, he was back on his feet again. Guy also stood when his client entered the room.

"Why do you stay so long in Morocco?" asked the client. "Most soldiers can't wait to leave."

"I like the heat: and the army are happy that I like the heat. I like the food and coffee. It suits us both, so I stay."

"You like the kif too, eh?" The client smiled.

Walter looked back at him politely, giving nothing away.

"Sit" the client said in a way that sounded like a question, as well as an offer- and an order too.

Walter sat, and noticed that Guy had left the room, which was good because it meant Walter didn't need to keep an eye on him. He didn't like Guy. Walter had found him to be arrogant on both occasions he'd met him at the bar.

Walter looked at the client. He was a sophisticated gentleman in his fifties, dressed in all white, his cotton shirt open at the neck but no gauche jewellery to be seen. He was smaller than Walter, and slim, with a full head of white hair that was oiled and brushed back smoothly, and his white eyebrows stood out from his dark skin. He looked rich but not dangerous. Walter thought he looked like Omar Sharif.

"My name is Omar" he said.

Walter smiled broadly and shook the hand offered to him.

"Let me tell you a short story, and then I'll tell you why you're here," said Omar.

"If you wish to stay and talk after my story, then we will do so, over lunch. If not, you leave and don't come back."

It wasn't a question; these were the rules, so Walter nodded and listened.

"I will be concise," said Omar. "In Switzerland, Zurich, to be precise, lives a man called Weber. I think you already know about him, is that right?" He raised his eyebrows and Walter nodded.

"He is a banker who has stolen a lot of money from me. To help you understand how this is possible, Mr. Mack, let me, without being patronising, explain about the kinds of useful banking services- which may be of interest to you soon- that are available in Switzerland. Account names do not exist: only numbers and codes. Anyone can keep money in those banks in Switzerland. It is not every bank in Switzerland that is like that Mr. Mack, just a few. All money kept in those few banks is there because outwardly law- abiding citizens from many countries wish to avoid paying tax. This of course means that they are not law- abiding citizens at all. And some people who keep their money in those banks do so for other reasons, mostly because they have come by that money through illegal means. And I include myself in that. You don't want to know how. We will never speak of that. The esteemed list of clients those banks have include Nazis, dependents of Nazis, the families of Nazis, friends of Nazis, organised crime, and a host of solitary individuals from arms traders to gamblers, international prostitutes and many white collar criminals.

So, from the very, very bad, to the not so bad- just a little bad. Legally, the authorities in Switzerland and in every country around the world have no right to access those accounts or know who the account holders are. The money is accessible at any time from any country you wish and the source of the income- how the money is made – well, no one ever knows, including the bank. And finally, the money is safe. It makes interest each year and it can be moved out of these private accounts for any purpose, again, without the source of income being divulged."

He hesitated, thinking he was perhaps talking too much.

"There's a little more to it than that, but not much. Does it make sense so far?"

Walter nodded.

"This banker I mentioned, Weber, managed to get access to my money via someone who worked for me, and the two of them stole it. They have also taken money from friends of mine. This was about a year ago. Since then, we have managed to recover the money so, financially, we're in good shape."

"What about the man who used to work for you?" asked Walter.

"Well, he lived here in Morocco, and he was persuaded to facilitate the return of the money, but unlike our financial situation, he is now not in good shape."

"I understand," said Walter.

"But the money is not of importance. Weber just did it for fun. However, he is behind two other problems which anger me greatly. The first is that he is starting to tread on my toes in business terms, by building or buying clubs and bars near where I have mine in Spain and here, in Morocco. Worst of all, he's financing this activity by trafficking people. Most of them young people. Children. I have a daughter. I can put up with most criminal activities, but not this."

"So, what is it that you want me to do?" asked Walter, choosing to make no comment on what Omar had said.

"I, and my friends, need for Weber to pay with his life for stealing from us and encroaching on my business. If we don't, then others will see us as weak. More importantly, to me, his treatment of young people is inhuman and his arrogance in thinking he can continue living a happy life in Switzerland is astonishing.

I want you to kill him. I have done a lot of my own homework on you, Walter, and I have heard much about you through various people, including your Colonel McLellan. You will be paid into a Swiss bank account – not Weber's of course."

Omar laughed at that because he thought the idea funny.

"I can help you open an account and show you how to use it. You can kill Weber by rifle if you choose to because it would be easy for you, and the safest method. I understand you can hit a bullseye from half a mile out."

Omar abruptly finished speaking and gestured to Walter with open hands. It was his turn to talk.

"Let's eat, Omar. I need to understand more, and I will need some help, but I will do the job. I will need a gun of a make and specifications which I will give you, left for me in Switzerland. This will be for you to arrange. I will need time. I need to resign from the army, and I have to serve notice. I will not desert. I need to go to Zurich. I need to spec the job out before killing Weber. I need to watch the man, learn his habits, watch his home. And somehow, I need to know that you're definitely going to pay me. Finally, I need to know if killing him will anger anyone else. I don't want people chasing me."

"I will explain everything after our lunch," said Omar. "Everything will be fine. Come on, I'm happy; and your good decision has made me hungry. Let's eat, and we'll talk again afterwards. First, I will introduce you to my daughter who'll join us for lunch: the beautiful Prudence."

During lunch, Walter's thoughts moved between the present and the future. How would he ensure he wasn't caught? Would there be any ramifications later? As for the present, one thing was for sure, Omar was accurate in describing his daughter Prudence as beautiful. Walter smiled at her from time to time, the smile she returned took his breath away. She had green eyes and shoulder-length unkempt blonde hair which fit perfectly with her dark skin and confident character. She wore a simple white dress.

"Walter, I'm over here." said Omar.

"I'm so sorry," said Walter. "I didn't mean to stare at Prudence. I was just admiring her hair and the colour of her eyes."

"Walter, I'm over here," said Prudence. "If you want to talk about my eyes and hair, you can ask me."

Walter blushed.

"Don't worry," Omar said smiling. "I'll explain. Prudence's mother, who walked out on us many years ago, was Italian. Italian women are like that." Prudence muttered something to herself, her now red face questioning the validity of her Father's sweeping statement.

"Luckily the only thing Prudence has inherited from her mother is the colour of her hair and eyes, and not her difficult nature. She has my beautiful skin and good nature."

Walter found that remark wholly bizarre but said nothing and gave nothing away. Given that Omar had just been discussing his plan to have someone murdered it was very odd.

"You both speak fabulous English," he said. "Where did you learn it?"

Prudence interrupted her father, who had just started to answer.

"Boarding school and university for me, in England, but thankfully all that's done. My father learned his English in prison in England, though I imagine that the institution I went to and the one he went to were quite similar."

"That's plenty, thank you my dear," said Omar, scowling at Prudence. He spoke again.

"When I was your age, Walter, I left my hardworking, yet chronically poor parents to travel around Europe, doing whatever I could to make money along the way. I ended up growing marijuana in glass houses for Romanians living outside London. I was arrested one day along with perhaps thirty other people and was sent to prison for three years. I served eighteen months. It was the best thing that could have happened to me. I learned English and I met Spanish people who to this day remain friends, indeed the very friends who are as angry with our Swiss friend as

I am. We bonded, we trusted each other, and we built businesses that flourish throughout northern Africa and southern Spain."

"Are any of them legal?" asked Prudence with a straight face.

"Yes, you know they are," replied Omar. "My daughter knows everything about me and my life" said Omar as he looked gravely towards Walter. The young Scotsman noted the mood of the conversation was changing. "I never hide anything," said Omar.

"Yes, you do. You hide most things," corrected Prudence.

"Some small things only," retorted Omar, "and if you know about them then I haven't hidden them very well."

"Rightly or wrongly, I tell my daughter most things, Walter, and I leave her to judge me as she sees fit. I'd rather have her judge me harshly than think that I lie to her."

"What kinds of things don't you tell her?" asked Walter. He was thinking about Switzerland.

"He didn't tell me that he has me followed when I go out at night," said Prudence, again jumping in before her father. "I'd known for a long time before I told him that I knew. But he worries about my safety. Rich people's children often go missing here so I understand why he does it. I also don't lie to him. He knows I have boyfriends."

Omar rolled his eyes.

"And I know that you're here about a man, somewhere outside of Morocco, Walter," said Prudence. "I know you're going to kill him."

Walter stopped eating and put his knife and fork down.

That statement shook him. A minute before, he was thinking he could fall in love with Prudence, and now he was wondering if she was as crooked as her father.

Prudence was staring at him.

"Walter, I know what you're thinking. I do. But I've heard of this man. He's ruined hundreds of lives, most of them children. We're not crazy. We know it's not right to kill someone, but in this case it's truly justified. A man with so much money and power would never end up going to prison. This is the only way. Don't think badly of me: remember, you're the one who's agreed to kill him."

"Ah yes, the power of logic," said Walter. "Good point. We're all in on this. Would you have contacted me if he hadn't been a danger to your bars and clubs?" he asked them both.

Omar said nothing, but Prudence nodded. "I would."

Walter noted the difference, picked up his knife and fork and resumed eating.

The next three months in Marrakech were just as transformative for Walter as the past six years in the army had been. The only dull thing had been serving his notice, although the planning of his trip to Switzerland was relatively boring too. It wasn't complicated. He simply had to go to Zurich, collect the rifle and bullets he had ordered from a pre-arranged collection point- a baggage storage unit at Zurich train station- then kill Weber, when and wherever he wished. He would likely be in Switzerland for three months or more as he studied Weber and his routines, then worked out the best vantage point from which to shoot him, but this wouldn't be hard work. He simply needed to make sure that he attracted as little attention as possible.

What took up most of Walter's time and headspace was Prudence. The strongest emotions he'd previously felt in his short lifetime were fear, abandonment, and loneliness; mixed with feelings of distrust and anger. Now, he felt something different. He thought constantly about Prudence, and while it felt like a loss of control, it also intrigued him. He'd never felt anything like this. It was all new, and pretty good.

<u>Chapter 9. Mixed Elves.</u>

During his notice period of three months, which he'd initially hoped he could avoid serving, but would end up glad that he did, he went into town often and walked the markets and the bars which he loved. Shortly after meeting Prudence at her father's home, he'd met her again by chance as he stopped for coffee one morning at a café close to the spice market. He saw her sitting across the square and waved, but she didn't see him. He stopped where he was, just to look at her and he felt his stomach lurch. She was beautiful. He admired the confidence with which she sat looking out at the people, it was exactly what he also liked to do; people watching. A much older man sat with her though, and this saddened Walter. While he watched, Prudence spotted Walter and smiled – and it was as if she'd come to life- she waved wildly at him and beckoned him over. His heart soared and he strode over making every effort to appear calm.

"Walter, hello. Sit," she said, motioning to the chair her companion sat in. The man got up and moved, standing at the side of the table. Walter motioned to the man to stay, but Prudence said, "No, you're not being rude, Walter; he's security- it's his job, he doesn't mind." She smiled at the man, who patted Walter on the shoulder to show that he wasn't offended. Walter sat, then he and Prudence began to talk.

He was going to ask what she was doing in town, but she beat him to it, and he answered:

"I like this café, and some others near here too. I come here often just to sit and look at the people and drink good coffee. The croissants and patisseries are awful, which is a shame. People watching is like reading a book. Don't you ever look at someone and wonder what their life is like? You know; where they live, who their cousins are, who their friends are, where they work, what they like to eat."

"That's so funny Walter, me too. But I find Marrakech stifling. And yet it's my world. Perhaps I spend too much time wondering and not enough time doing. It's stifling, and I don't mean stifling hot, it's just too confined here. There's a whole world out there. What do you think?"

For the next hour, Walter and Prudence conversed constantly, and during this time Walter found himself relaxing in her company. He did wonder briefly if she only spoke with him because she knew that he'd be soon on his way to Switzerland, and he was now in business with her father. Was this a business meeting he was having? It was odd too, that she spoke so freely with him about so many things and yet she knew he was soon to commit murder. She seemed to be so relaxed, and the more she spoke, the more interested he became in hearing what she had to say. She was incredibly interesting and was, he eventually decided, genuinely interested in him. She asked about his past but not in a way that felt intrusive.

Whenever he felt himself liking her too much though, he was brought back to his reality by the knowledge that she was the daughter of someone very unpleasant. That said, his own mother wasn't any great shakes. Prudence was genuine, he was pretty sure. His heart was playing a role here though, not just his head. He decided that he'd stop thinking so much and lower his guard just a little to enjoy her company, not question it.

He smiled at her. She smiled back.

"When do you leave, Walter?"

"Soon, two and a half months from today to be precise."

"Oh. I didn't know. I thought it might be later. Will you come back to Marrakech? I don't even know where you're going. Can you tell me?"

"I can't, I'm sorry. It's the way these things work – I'm sure you understand."

Prudence nodded because she did indeed understand.

"Wherever I'm going, I'll need to leave there too within a month or so of arriving and go somewhere else, but I don't know where yet. I'll work that out soon. I'm thinking about it." He was becoming a little cagey with this line of questioning. So much for dropping his guard.

"I'm just asking Walter, I'm interested. I'm not asking on behalf of my father."

Walter smiled at her again. And she smiled at him again.

"You're interested?"

"Yes, I am. Why are you so surprised?"

Walter didn't know how to answer that without embarrassing himself.

From then on, every day, Walter and Prudence met at the same café at the same time and spoke until they couldn't drink any more coffee or eat any more bad pastries.

For the first time in his life, he spoke to another person about his mother. He told her how as a boy she'd constantly tell him the story of when she was young. She woke up excited on her birthday, wondering what her parents had in store for her. As the day progressed, she realised that they'd forgotten. She had said that the incident stayed with her all her life.

Cut forward to Walter's fourteenth birthday. He woke up, just as his mother had, knowing it was his birthday, similarly excited.. And of course, his parents had forgotten. Right up until late evening he had expected a surprise, and it never came. It was a bad enough experience for a young boy but coming after years of listening to his mother tell the same story of herself, it seemed impossible. Unless of course it was done on purpose.

"I can't think of anything sadder," said Prudence, "I'm so sorry to hear such a thing Walter. If we lived in the same city, I'd never forget your birthday. Ever. And we'd go out and celebrate it every year. I can't understand how something like that could happen. I'm from a family of crooks and murderers and they're not as heartless as that. Poor you."

The next day, when Walter arrived at the café for coffee, a birthday cake was sitting on the table in front of Prudence.

"Happy birthday, Walter."

He laughed. "It's not my birthday."

"I guess not, but I don't know when it is. So today, we change the rules. Today is your birthday and I'm taking you out all day and all night. First, we eat cake."

She motioned for the waiter who brought out two plates and two forks with coffee. Prudence passed a camera to the bodyguard who took a photograph of them together, smiling at the camera. They sat close to each other, and he could smell her hair.

As they'd do every time they met prior to Walter's departure, they touched feet under the table, often, but not in a flirty way; it was their version of holding hands. It was just something they did. Walter loved it and took to not wearing socks. This simple act, possibly silly to some people, was the most intimate thing Walter had ever experienced. He'd feel the protective wall that guarded him against being let down beginning to crumble, but not completely.

Prudence and Walter each ate a slice of the birthday cake then Prudence looked Walter in the eye and said: "Happy Birthday."

Walter stood and excused himself from the table. Prudence watched him walk towards the market and stop, hands on hips, staring at the sky. He was taking deep breaths, but shortly returned to his seat.

Prudence reached out and placed her hand on top of his.

"Are you alright?"

"I've never been better." It was absolutely true.

Lunch was spent at a small restaurant that Prudence knew just on the outskirts of the city, and the three of them- security was always close by- spent lunchtime eating figs, beef, couscous, anchovies and chicken; all spiced, and each mouthful an experience in itself. It put to shame the drab food that Walter had endured growing up.

As evening approached, they went to the Pale Moon Bar where Prudence knew everyone. It was an interesting crowd- all Moroccan it seemed, yet everyone westernised in manner and dress, drinking vermouth and gin, speaking in Arabic, French and English.

"Walter, pay attention," said Prudence, "I am going to make you the best drink you have ever had. It is something that I invented myself, and I never tell anyone what the ingredients are. But, since today is your birthday, or my birthday for you, I'm going to tell you, but only after you try it."

And with that said, she went behind the bar as if she owned the place (perhaps she did, thought Walter) and she went to work making their drinks, which when done, were served in tall straight glasses, ice cold.

Walter accepted his gracefully and was about to sip it when Prudence stopped him.

"To you, again, Walter. Happy birthday!"

This was kindness of a type he'd never experienced before, and it was hard for Walter to take it in his stride. He struggled to contain himself. Fighting was easy for him, being cared for was not.

"Be happy Walter, it's a day of celebration." Prudence kissed him on the lips and ruffled his hair. He blushed.

"What do you call this drink?" he asked before sipping it. He was keen to change the subject quickly.

"Mixed Elves."

"That's probably the oddest name I've ever heard for a drink. What does it mean, how did you come up with that name?"

"I honestly don't know," she said. "One night I just dreamt the name- it was a dream I had about being with friends and being happy, and we were all drinking these cocktails called Mixed Elves. When I woke, I asked people if they'd ever heard of them, but no one had. Somehow the name had just come to me in the night, and I liked it because it was so unusual. It's mysterious and a little odd- like me."

Walter sipped his drink and was taken aback. It was fabulous. It had the same powerful kick as a good Martini, but even more refreshing. It wasn't a drink, it was a hit, but easily drinkable: thoroughly dangerous he thought. Brilliant. He could taste gin, lemon, sparkling water, definitely: perhaps sugar- but there was a lot more and he couldn't quite identify any of the other ingredients. It had taken Prudence about five minutes to make them which seemed like quite a lot of work, but well worth it he thought.

"What's in it? It's great."

Prudence leaned forward and whispered in his ear: and he listened carefully. It was a very complicated recipe, but he'd never forget what she told him.

"To Prudence," he toasted. "My mixed elf."

"To us, Walter- mixed elves."

That evening was the best that Walter could ever remember. So much, yet so little had happened. He'd simply shared an evening with Prudence, but fallen in love for the first time and, he was sure, the only time in his life he ever would.

On his last visit to Omar, to finalise arrangements, two days before he left for Switzerland, the two sat together in the vast living room and talked business. Walter had waited until a significant deposit had been placed in his new bank account in Zurich before he'd resigned from the army. All was in place now, and as today's meeting covered final details around collecting the custom-made rifle: it would also be their last meeting.

"One final thing," said Omar. "Remember this. You're not going to kill a good man. He is bad. So don't have second thoughts. And second, you'll never see myself or Prudence again. However, I want to wish you luck for the future."

It was bad news, confirmed. It wasn't a surprise, but for something that wasn't a surprise it hurt him badly to hear it. Walter didn't reply or nod his head either; he didn't want to.

He hadn't seen Prudence when he'd arrived at the house that morning, but he was due to see her the following day for coffee. He had decided to tell her where he was going and how she could contact him- and how he planned to write to her when he was settled. In his mind he wanted to leave Morocco knowing that he'd see her again within twelve weeks, ideally somewhere in Europe. But before then he'd telephone her.

He didn't want to be too pushy, because being Walter, he wasn't completely sure how she felt about him. He knew that she cared for him, but did she care for him as much as he did for her? Love was new territory for Walter. Tomorrow's rendezvous with her would be the most important one of his life.

Chapter 10. Walter's last day, Marrakech.

Prudence and Walter had planned to spend his last day and night together, but she didn't turn up at the café at the appointed time. There was no message left for him. He waited for two hours before he stood, paid the bill and left. He went back to base and packed. He looked at his hammer and the words carved on the handle before putting it into his bag; "your fault." He felt like hitting himself between the eyes with it. It was true. The words were written for those he had used the hammer on in the past, but today they could be written for himself. He was a fool. She could have anyone in the world. Why would she want him?

He felt foolish for telling her that everyone he'd ever trusted had let him down. He was setting himself up.

He sat down on the little wooden chair in his sparse room and took a piece of writing paper out of the little desk. He planned to write a letter to Prudence. He would enclose the photograph taken of the two of them the day she celebrated his birthday. He'd been tempted to vent his anger in the letter, to ask how she could do such a thing. He felt the same hollow feeling he'd felt when his mother had forgotten his birthday, but as the hours passed, he shook that feeling off and decided he needed to grow up. He was being weak, and he was no longer a child. So, he chose instead to write on the back of the photograph what he truly felt. He put the photograph in an envelope and posted it that evening. He'd simply written "My happiest day ever."

That night he dreamt the recurring dream and slept even more poorly than usual.

By midmorning the following day, he was on a military flight back to England. Once in England he made his way to Heathrow and boarded a flight to Switzerland, steeled, back to his usual self, and ready to kill.

Chapter 11. Zurich, December 1976.

The view from Walter's window seat on the plane was stunning. He felt so close to the top of the Swiss Alps that he could step out of the plane onto a mountain top. The sun shone brightly, and the sky was a dark blue, not the light blue of summer, but equally as beautiful. It lifted Walter's spirits. He was well used to disappointment- it had been the one steady factor throughout his life- but his unnecessary disposal at the hands of Prudence seemed punitive, not just uncaring. She was strong, so if she hadn't been at the café for their last meeting, it would have been her choice, not her father's.

He wondered if there was any truth in the saying "what doesn't kill you makes you stronger" because he felt it might be more accurate to say: "what doesn't kill you makes you incredibly angry."

He tried to focus on the job at hand. Weber was astonishingly evil, and either arrogant or dimwitted if he thought that the matter would be closed once Omar had his money back. Perhaps he wrongly assumed that the distance between Zurich and Marrakech protected him. Whatever the reason, it wasn't Walter's problem.

Once inside a taxi, he headed straight to Zurich HB train station. Shortly after, he arrived outside the imposing and grand main entrance and having seen so little of the city on the way there, he decided that he'd stretch his legs after checking into his pre-booked and pre-paid long stay apartment.

Everything he'd had to do at Zurich HB had gone smoothly. He already had the key to the locker in the station and on opening it, found that it contained a large travel bag which fitted inside the locker and no more. t felt just about the right weight when he pulled it out, and after throwing it over his shoulder he went back to the taxi rank with his travel bag from Morocco across his other shoulder, he set off for the apartment in another taxi. The key for the apartment had also been in the locker waiting for him which meant that no check in was required.

On taking a lift to the fifth floor of the building and entering the apartment he found a small living room, a bathroom, and a bedroom with a large safe inside the walk-in closet. The safe did not belong to the owners of the apartment building. It had been placed there by contacts of Omar's. Walter used the code which was in an envelope inside the bag he collected at the train station, and then memorised it, burnt it, then opened the safe. As planned, the safe was large enough to take the bag he'd collected at the train station. He opened the bag and found the rifle he'd ordered, broken down into parts which he would rebuild. Spreading the parts out on the double bed, he looked at them and on inspecting them found himself satisfied. He needed a coffee before starting the task of putting the gun together. He had to build the rifle, deconstruct it and rebuild it many times before aiming it at Weber. It was crucial that he test the gun and know that he could pull it to pieces in seconds after squeezing the trigger. It would be a key part of his speedy get away and disposal of evidence.

The apartment was Swiss- sparse, and immaculately clean. Crisp white sheets covered the bed, and a dull grey carpet was laid out throughout the whole space. The kitchen was functional, and some initial supplies had been left for him, including coffee, an Italian espresso pot, milk and sugar. Perfect. The living room had a sofa, a television, a coffee table, a writing desk and a chair. He made himself coffee then sat on the rock- hard sofa, taking in his surroundings. The window in the living room looked onto the side of the building adjacent which was good, because while Walter had no real view, no one could see him or into his apartment. He could barely see the sky above him because his building was so close to the next. It was beautifully anonymous and highly functional. He made his coffee, downed it, then went back through to the bedroom to put his custom-made rifle together and map out the next few days ahead.

Chapter 12. Jacob.

The rifle was superb. Walter had provided a detailed spec to Omar in Marrakech, and it had been followed expertly, resulting in a beautifully balanced gun with two dozen bullets. Used correctly, Weber would be killed with one clean shot. Plenty of spares for practice.

Walter spent the next day walking the snowy streets of Zurich on what was Christmas Eve. He bought a good map of the city and another of the entire country which he would use in planning his shot and finding a place to practice. On his way back to his apartment late in the afternoon he felt the urge for a drink, and perhaps the company of people. The apartment was perfect, but like a prison cell. Walter wasn't keen on talking to others, but he liked people nearby. Up ahead of him as he walked was a bar, and the yellow glow from the lighting inside looked warm and welcoming. He pushed the door open and stepped inside to find it empty except for the barman, an old man with thin white hair. He was unshaven and looked ill. Walter unwound the newly purchased wool scarf from his neck, unbuttoned his long black coat and sat at the bar. He hadn't shaved, so stubble covered his chin. His lips had cracked from the cold. Looking for company, it looked as if Walter had chosen the only bar in Zurich with no one in it, and on Christmas Eve too.

The barman said something to him in German, so Walter shook his head and replied in English, saying he was sorry, but he only spoke English.

The barman smiled and said "It's not a problem young man. I speak good English too. What would you like to drink?"

"Red wine, please."

"Not beer? Red wine is an unusual choice of drink for a young man."

"Well, I tend to only drink beer in warm places."

"I have wine, so you'll be fine," the barman said. "That rhymes nicely."

"Oh dear," thought Walter. That was a bad sign, surely. He'd better give himself a few minutes to warm up, drink his wine and then leave.

"I'm Jacob," said the barman.

"Nice to meet you, Jacob," said Walter and held out his hand. They shook.

"Are you going to tell me your name?" asked Jacob.

"Ely," replied Walter, thinking for no logical reason of one of the French soldiers he was stationed with.

"Ah, you're Jewish, good." said Jacob.

"No, I'm not," said Walter.

"It's most unusual for people who are not Jewish to name their child Ely."

"My parents were unusual."

"Are you from Zurich?" said Walter, keen to change the subject.

"Berlin" said Jacob.

"What brought you to Zurich?"

"The Holocaust."

Over several glasses of wine, Walter heard much about the Holocaust that he didn't know. Jacob described how his family had fled Berlin when it became clear that at some point they were going to be arrested and transported away. He told Walter how it took such a long time for the feeling of disbelief about what was happening to turn to realisation, despite the horror around them every day. The change to acceptance of the reality was terrifying, as was the knowledge that no one was going to save them. So, they fled, but didn't even make it out of Berlin. Almost all of Jacob's family died, all of them separated from each other when jammed into the trains that took them east to the concentration camps. His parents, brother, wife and one son all died. Jacob told Walter how he'd given up on God and humanity while he was interned. He couldn't understand how he had survived because he didn't really want to survive. Perhaps he had an inbuilt level of stamina that others didn't have. He really didn't know. He lost half of his body weight but didn't get sick. He was close to the prime of his life, and strong, aged forty, so that would have helped. As the weight dropped off him, and everyone else too, he considered suicide as many had done before him, but something- to this day he didn't know what- kept him going. Every day he'd get out of his lice-ridden bunk and clean the guards' toilets as was his job, all day, every day.

"Did you ever regain your faith in humanity?" asked Walter.

"I don't know- I left internment confused."

"Confused in what way?"

"About a year or so before we were eventually released, a German guard started inspecting my hut at night. Contrary to rules, many of the huts were mixed- mixed ethnicity, mixed sex, mixed ages. The guards had just started putting anyone into any hut and not segregating them. There were parentless children in mine who'd lie huddled together on a bed or on the floor. As this one particular guard walked around the hut in the dark at night- supposedly counting heads- I noticed that as he passed the children, lumps of bread and scraps of meat would fall out of the leg of his trousers. The guard had cut holes in his pockets so he could surreptitiously let the food roll down his trouser leg and onto the floor. The children would pounce on it, and the adults never had a chance of getting any of it, because the guard made sure to be standing beside the children whenever he released the food. I would watch this from my bunk at the back of the hut, just able to see and no more in the dark hell that was the hut. That, I have to say, gave me a little hope. The hope may even have kept me alive. That guard risked his life doing what he did, and he certainly saved some young lives; no doubt about that.

Time dragged on and the guard continued doing this until eventually the camp was freed. We had no access to news from the outside world, so it was a complete surprise when it happened. It was Russian soldiers who freed us. They just opened the gates and let us through. It was a cold, sunny day, and all of a sudden, we were free with absolutely no idea of what to do or where to go. In the chaos that followed the freeing of the prisoners, the Russians rounded up the guards, all of whom had surrendered. I watched as they shot them, one by one, including the man who had fed and saved the children. Everyone who was still alive watched. No one from my hut who knew what this guard had done for the children spoke up for him. And to my shame, nor did I. And I don't know why. I really don't. The man didn't ask for help from any of the prisoners; he didn't plead. He stood quietly in the snow, right beside the gates to freedom as they put a gun to his head and shot him. I think he'd tired of being alive. For many years after, I thought about that man and felt guilty for not speaking up, but over time I learned to live with it. I could barely stand when I saw what happened to him, far less intervene, but it was no excuse for saying nothing. Eventually, years later, I woke one morning, said a prayer for that man, and then moved on with my life, with one son who had also survived. I needed to find peace. I couldn't save that guard, but I could now save myself. What had happened was part of my journey. Not moving on would have wasted what the man had done. I was still alive and lucky to be so. Today I use that experience to give me perspective. I expect nothing in life except some effort from myself, and to learn from experiences. You know, Ely, just because you do the right thing, doesn't mean that the right thing's going to happen to you."

Jacob, sighed, and with a smile, turned to the gantry and pulled a whisky for both himself and Walter. He handed Walter one, and toasted: "To the sanctity of life." They clinked glasses.

"And so, what are you doing in Zurich?" asked Jacob.

Chapter 13. Ibex.

The middle of winter wasn't the best time of the year for doing the kind of job that Walter had to do in Zurich. People walked less and drove more. They didn't drink outside and didn't use their gardens. There was less light, and it was freezing cold and windy, which all made Walter's testing of the rifle a harder task than he'd have liked. He needed the expanse of the mountain areas to practice, which annoyingly happened to be the only place that people did go in great numbers, and that was for skiing. He had to find space and test the rifle- no question- so he hired a car on a Tuesday, thinking that there wouldn't be too many people around on a work day, and drove out of the city past Lake Zurich and towards the beautiful Mount Rigi.

He'd packed a bag for the day with sandwiches and a flask of coffee, as well as the rifle. He'd need to trek quite a distance from where he parked, away from hotels, lodges – indeed, anywhere that people might be, in order to find the level of peace he needed. He was dressed for the job so there was no question of being unprepared for difficult terrain or any danger of freezing. He just needed to avoid being seen when he tested the rifle. It could be silenced so he wouldn't be heard and wouldn't cause any avalanches if he happened to end up higher in the mountains than he wanted to be. Two hundred yards was the distance he felt would work best for him to kill Weber; near enough to be sure of hitting his target, and far enough away to be out of sight and not get caught up in the panic that would possibly follow the shooting. He still had to follow Weber and get to know his habits, something he'd initially planned to do before testing the rifle so he could gauge the distance, but he'd changed his mind and was now keen to ensure he had the right equipment first, otherwise he could waste weeks. After testing the equipment, he'd get to know Weber's habits, test the equipment again after choosing his spot- then kill him.

With everything packed for the hike, he left his car and followed the trail on his map, walking for two hours. His six years in Morocco had left him exceptionally fit, so the walk was easy for him, despite the climb. He left the trail he was on and ventured out over terrain that wasn't snow-covered and wasn't easily accessible because of rock formations and rubble, which meant there was only a small chance of coming across any people. After another thirty minutes, he found the perfect spot. Sheltering under a pine tree, he sat on his rucksack and ate his sandwiches and drank his coffee, admiring the serenity and beauty that surrounded him. The sky was dark grey but the visibility, still good. There was a breeze which he judged to be around fifteen miles per hour, per the forecast. That was likely more than on the day he would choose to carry out the shooting, but it was fine for practice.

After putting his flask and sandwich wrapping away, he walked south and paced out two hundred yards downhill, giving him similar elevation to that he thought he might have on the day. He was probably going to be aiming from inside a building and down to the street. On the day, it'd be likely that Weber would be walking. Walter had decided that he wasn't going to shoot him if he was close to others.

He stopped walking and stooped down to pick up a rock the size of a small football and placed it on top of a larger boulder before walking back to where his rucksack lay. He pieced the rifle together and lay down on the ground preparing to take aim at the small rock that sat downhill. As he did, he saw a solitary male ibex come into view, its huge horns looking as if they weighed more than the animal itself. It was the breeding season, and usually males sporting beards would travel together in small groups, but this one was on its own, possibly having just lost a rut. On its back was a bird that looked to be grooming it for parasites. The ibex now grazed beside the boulder that Walter had just placed, and this gave him an unexpected opportunity. Having set the rifle on its tripod, he took aim at the bird. With an exact spot in sight, he squeezed the trigger and the rifle bounced slightly. There was a quiet, muffled pop. His eye stayed glued to the telescope, and he watched as the unfortunate bird exploded in a cloud of feathers. The ibex was startled and bolted uphill towards Walter, unaware of his presence. It came nearer and nearer to where he lay. The wind was blowing uphill, and Walter could smell the Ibex as it approached, but the Ibex couldn't smell him. Walter wondered if he should stay or move to avoid getting trampled, but it veered to the left and passed him by a good twenty yards, before eventually slowing down then stopping.

The gun was good. No need to use another bullet. Walter packed up, pleased to be finishing earlier than he thought he would, then walked back to his car at a brisk pace. He got there a good hour before darkness fell and turned on the heater then poured himself another coffee from his flask, pleased to be out of the chill breeze, and enjoying the cold mountain outside from the warmth inside. He'd had a good day, so he'd go for a walk after dinner and drop into one of the chocolate box bars for a drink. Maybe Jacob's. He turned on the headlights, started the engine then made for Zurich.

Chapter 14. Xander. January 1977.

Sitting inside Jacob's bar again, Walter was deep in conversation with him. It was difficult conversing with Jacob when he had to consistently lie about the most mundane of things, but he liked the old man's company. Jacob never pried though, and Walter never gave away too much. But he did tell him about his desire to be a chef, something he'd only spoken to Prudence about in detail. And he told Jacob about his mother lying unconscious on the floor snoring as he vaguely considered- briefly- revising for exams. He talked of the cold and wet of his Edinburgh home. One of his childhood pals once claimed in jest that he'd been inside Walter's house, and it had been so cold indoors that it was snowing. His experiences paled into insignificance when he'd heard what Jacob had been through of course, and at times Walter felt like a moaning wimp. There was a degree of commonality between the two men though, and that was experiencing the misery the world could heap upon its people in all sorts of ways. Walter wondered how Jacob could be such a relaxed and genial old man given what he'd gone through. Perhaps Walter's problems lay with Walter, not everyone else? His judgement of people had been pretty good over the years, he felt, except for Prudence of course. Her not being there on his last day in Morocco had taken him by surprise.

That night, Jacob's grandson, Xander was helping him behind the bar despite the fact that once again, it was quiet. Beautiful festive music played in the background. It was the kind of German music that everyone in Britain thinks is British. Walter was sitting on a bar stool looking round, soaking up the warm yellow lighting, the candles and the smell of cigars and cigarettes.

He and Jacob spoke more; and again, Walter veered the conversation away from himself when things became too personal. He was caught off guard, though, when Jacob asked if he had a love in his life. Walter blushed. Jacob saw this and laughed out loud.

"Is she here, in Zurich?'

"No, not here; a long way away. I won't see her again. It's over. Done."

"My goodness Walter, that sounds very, very final. What went wrong?"

"She did." He went on to explain in a roundabout way how close they'd become, he believed, and even though they'd never slept together, it felt as though they had. Circumstances had dictated that they were never really alone. The last night they had planned would have changed that. He had never felt anything like it before.

"It's called love, Walter."

"As I say, I'd never felt anything like it before."

"And why didn't she turn up for your last rendezvous?"

"I imagine because I was leaving to travel, and therefore she decided that there would be no point, I suppose."

"She told you this?"

"No, I never saw her again, or heard from her."

"Walter, there could be a million reasons why she wasn't there. You're very negative. You don't know why she wasn't there."
Jacob expanded. "Perhaps she was run over on the way there, or she was ill. You don't know. You're very hard on her, and maybe yourself too. You should write to her."

"No."

"Are you saying no because you don't want to feel let down again if you don't get an answer, or perhaps you are frightened that you'll get an answer you don't like?"

Walter said nothing.

Jacob leaned over and patted the younger man on the shoulder. "You must have had a hard past Walter- you're so used to seeing the worst in people and life. But keep going and try to be a little more positive. There are some good people too. Don't just assume the worst. Maybe your future will be with Prudence after all, but if not, it will be someone else. Walter, it feels to me that your approach to life has you permanently standing in the rain without an umbrella. You need to move. Walk into the sunshine."

Chapter 15. Weber.

The following day, Walter began to watch Weber from a distance. He saw him arrive at the bank in the morning- he didn't leave for lunch- saw him leave that evening at five thirty pm and walk across the road to an underground car park then drive out shortly afterwards. Sitting on a scooter, frozen, Walter followed the car as sleet fell in the dark, headlights dazzling him as he moved behind Weber who headed slowly out of the business district and into the suburbs. Walter wanted to know about his target's habits, and so, for the next month he followed him, picking him up whenever he could, trying to avoid sitting for hours on end in the one spot. Already, he knew what time Weber arrived at his place of work, where he parked and, shortly he'd learn, where he'd recently moved. And over time, he'd know where he went at weekends, at nights, and he'd work out when and where to kill him with the least chance of being caught. Walter would be patient and meticulous. The army had trained him well.

As the weeks went by, he learned that Tuesday and Thursday evenings Weber went home, ate, bathed and changed, then took a taxi to a bar that was close to the city centre. It was discreet and unnamed, and looked from the outside more like the private office of a small business than a bar. Gathering intelligence was part of Walter's training and he also had a good gut feel, so he felt that this was no ordinary venue. He decided to go inside at some point but judging by the men who'd been going in as he watched, he'd need to get rid of the biking gear and get into civilian clothes.

So, he did just that, arriving at the bar at ten pm on a Thursday evening. It was a gay bar; something that surprised Walter a little, although he wasn't sure why. Switzerland was one of the most progressive countries in Europe. Perhaps it was simply the look of the place from the outside: dull and featureless. The venue was cavernous inside, and by the time Walter arrived, there were over fifty men of all ages spread around the bar- some on their own, some in groups- most of them flirting with someone.

At the rear of the venue, close to the cloakroom was Weber, talking to a much younger man. In person and up close, he was exactly as the various photos given to Walter had portrayed him: overweight, short, a lot of teeth showing, and dyed black hair combed to the side. He was immaculately turned out in a tweed jacket, black trousers and a Paisley cravat. It was unusual to find anyone wearing a cravat these days, thought Walter. It looked ridiculous. The younger man seemed to be enamoured with Weber, despite the cravat though, and he seemed to be hanging onto every word Weber spoke. Perhaps he was really enamoured with Weber's wealth.

Unfamiliar with this scene, Walter wondered how much people who met in a club like that would tell each other about themselves- or how much of it would be true. Perhaps most of them, like Weber, were married and so the less said, the better. He was about to leave because he'd found what he was looking for – the perfect spot to target Weber. Close to the entrance would work well. The street was quiet, and it would make it easy for Walter to get away at speed on a dark evening. Weber would continue to turn up at the same time, twice per week. That level of certainty was useful. When investigating the cause of Weber's death, it'd be likely the police would find out about his secret life, and spend time looking to see if somehow there could be a connection, such as a spurned lover; blackmail perhaps- or someone with a broken heart. The barman leant over and put a glass of red wine in front of Walter. Walter looked at it, then at the barman, and shook his head- not keen to speak, thereby divulging that he wasn't Swiss. The barman pointed behind Walter and there was Xander, sitting with someone around his own age. He smiled at Walter and waved, indicating that Walter should join them.

Walter cursed to himself; this was exactly the kind of coincidence that was most unwelcome.

He walked over to Xander and shook his outstretched hand, and the hand of his friend, who turned out to be named Kurt.

There were no questions about Walter's sexuality from the two young men but instead they talked about Kurt's music career- which had stalled according to Kurt- and never taken off according to Xander. Walter was ready to go as quickly as he could though, because the longer he spoke with people the more likely it was that a hole in his background story would show. After as short a period of time as he judged reasonable, he stood to go, offering to buy them both a drink before he did so. As luck would have it, they were ready to leave too. Walter sighed to himself. Could it get worse? Donning hats and scarves, the three of them left the table just as six skinheads entered the bar. They were there to cause trouble. English football fans visiting for a European cup football match in Zurich. This night was going about as badly as it could. Walter wondered if he'd bump into his mother outside.

Xander and Kurt had stopped hesitantly on seeing the skinheads, thinking it might be safer to go back but they had already been spotted by the skinheads who smelled blood. Walter told Kurt and Xander to keep going, pass the skinheads and leave, but it didn't work out as planned.

Walter was walking beside Kurt and Xander when the three of them were stopped. A conversation started in English. Although Xander and Kurt were much taller than Walter, they were the kind of people the skinheads loved to fight; fearful. The insults grew as the skinheads pushed for a fight and blocked the exit. They got louder and louder, and Walter hoped that at some point they'd stop and the three of them could get past without drawing any further attention to themselves. But despite efforts from the bar staff, it didn't look as if the skinheads were going to leave. Dressed in turned-up faded jeans, boots, braces and white T-shirts- no coats in freezing temperatures- they weren't going to leave until they'd inflicted damage.

Walter spoke for the first time, in English, using a thick German accent that the skinheads wouldn't detect as fabricated. He had no wish to be identified as British.

"Gents, we'd just like to leave. Let us past please."

"Listen to that," said the one who'd been shouting insults into Xander's face.

The skinhead repeated what Walter had said, mocking his German accent, and as he did so, he pulled a knife from his back pocket. Walter saw the knife and sank his forefinger deep into the man's eye, which from then on would be useless. The man dropped to his knees screaming, the knife on the floor beside him. Walter picked it up and turned to look at the others, as Xander and Kurt looked at him. Kurt, Xander and the skinheads stood where they were, unsure of what to do next.

Walter explained. "Keep your distance and do not follow us outside, or you will deeply regret your visit to Zurich. Goodbye." With a nudge, he motioned Xander and Kurt to the door.

Outside, a taxi was waiting for customers across the road. Walter told Xander and Kurt to get into the taxi then leave as fast as they could. The two men stood rooted to the spot, now keeping a distance from Walter, their faces ashen. It seemed that they were more frightened of him than they were of the skinheads. He understood their shock at what they'd just seen but he had no sympathy. He'd saved their skins.

"Shouldn't we call an ambulance?" asked Kurt.

"Not if you don't want to end up in jail, no. The barman will have called one. Leave right now. I'll walk home."

He turned up his collar and walked away, hearing the muffled footsteps of Xander and Kurt as they ran across the road and into the taxi. The door slammed and the taxi took off.

Chapter 16. A Change of plan.

Walter was furious with himself. He was sure that Weber hadn't noticed him or seen his face in the bar, but he would have been aware of what went on, so it was still possible. While it was highly unlikely that he'd connect Walter to Omar even if he had seen him, any attention was very unhelpful. He didn't regret how he had dealt with the skinhead because he didn't really have a choice, but he did regret the attention. Xander would tell Jacob what had happened- unless of course Xander wouldn't want to tell Jacob where he'd been. That was a real possibility, so hopefully things might not be quite as bad as he initially thought. Still, he needed to act with even more caution and finish the task ahead faster than he'd planned. The less time in Zurich now, the better. At least the skinheads wouldn't have identified Walter as British. They were idiots.

Back at his apartment, he poured himself a large whisky from the bottle he'd purchased on his way back and sat down to think and reboot his plan.

Weber's routines were pretty clear, holidays and business travel aside. In terms of a spot to do the job, the club had been a good find. Walter had decided early on that killing him outside his home just wasn't on. As much as he'd heard from Omar and McLellan how insidious a character the man was, Weber shouldn't be killed where his children might see the body. Killing him as he arrived or left the bar one Tuesday or Thursday evening would be best. Possibly his arrival would be best. When leaving, he might be with someone. Walter was convinced that the police would imagine there was a link to the bar and its customers, at least initially. It would certainly give him a little more time to leave Switzerland. The skinheads would leave for England as soon as their friend got out of hospital, likely within the next day or possibly two. Things would settle. Once again though, he reminded himself that absolute anonymity would have been better. He'd made a mistake in the bar. He should just have left instead of sitting down with Xander: perhaps pretended he was embarrassed. Going forward, he'd need to be more careful.

He thought about the bar and its location. He probably had about twenty seconds between the time that Weber would leave his taxi and the time he'd enter the bar. When Walter had watched, Weber's taxi had come from the east and stopped across the road from the bar. There was a church about a hundred yards from the bar, and it offered the perfect vantage point to take his shot. Walter would pace it out exactly. Gaining access to the church would be easy. He'd avoid the area for a week or so in case there was any residual police activity following the confrontation with the skinheads, then look at the church in more detail. From there, he'd probably choose the following Tuesday or Thursday evening, depending on the weather forecast. It needed to be dry, with as little wind as possible.

After that, his plan was to dispose of the rifle in parts, in Lake Zurich, then the following day board a train to Paris like many other backpackers. Once there, he'd rent a room, and work out exactly what he planned to do next. He still felt that training to be a chef would be the best option because it was the one thing that he really wanted to do. It was just as he'd told Jacob, but he needed to do a little more research on the subject because while he'd like to possess the skills of a chef, he wouldn't like to be employed as one. Of course, he kept forgetting that he wouldn't actually need to work, so worrying about working was a waste of time. It was about learning to do something he'd love in the future. It all needed some thought. He was excited about the change in his life though. It was as if one of his life's building blocks was fitting into place: financial security. Omar wouldn't renege on paying what he owed simply because he was rich, and it'd be bad business- not worth the fall out. He wouldn't want Walter looking for him.

As he waited a week, Walter spent the time looking for the right places around Lake Zurich to dispose of the rifle parts, and he travelled to the countryside to test out the rifle again, this time from a much greater height and from the distance he'd paced out from the church to the bar. He decided against going in to see Jacob one last time, which saddened him because he really liked the old man. There were so few people he liked. Jacob was interesting, and had been good to him, but with the risk that Xander had told him about the incident at the bar, he felt it would be asking for trouble.

Instead, he wrote a card which he'd post to Jacob as he left, wishing him well, saying that he had to leave for Britain suddenly due to a death in the family. Hopefully, somehow, he'd see Jacob again someday. He might even write to him in the upcoming months.

Two weeks later, with clear skies forecast for the evening, and just a light breeze, Walter readied himself for his task. He'd made a point of not getting to know anything more about Weber other than his work routine, for it would serve no purpose. Morally, Walter had had second thoughts, but only briefly because he'd simplified things in his mind: Weber was evil. Walter would prevent him from inflicting misery on others. The task at hand was also Walter's passport to freedom. He would need to bury this incident at the back of his mind the second he boarded the train to Paris.

The evening and the time came. Walter was in place in the church tower, scanning the bar's entrance and the pavement across the road through the rifle's telescopic lens. He'd been there from eight pm, setting up, expecting to see Weber sometime around nine or ten pm. At nine thirty pm, a taxi pulled up across the road from the bar and Weber got out. He stood on the pavement, looking both ways before deciding to cross the road. He stepped out, and seconds later, as his right foot touched the pavement on the opposite side of the road, his head exploded when Walter's bullet hit.

Within sixty seconds, Walter was out of the church; and within two minutes he was in his car driving carefully to his apartment. By the time he was in his apartment, the police had arrived at the scene and Walter was sipping a whisky, glad to feel the fire of it burn his throat. Despite everything he'd told himself leading up to this, it wasn't going to be so easy to forget.

He stayed inside his apartment for two days, then on the third, drove out to Lake Zurich where he disposed of the rifle parts in six different locations. On the way back he posted the card to Jacob, and by evening, having returned his rental car, he was on a train to Paris, dressed as a backpacker with a large rucksack behind him. He hadn't shaved for days, and he looked just the part.

<u>Chapter 17. Paris, Late January 1977.</u>

Having spent so much time in Morocco, and with French soldiers, Walter had eventually gained a basic understanding of the language by the time he arrived in Paris. It was not at all good, but good enough. He found grim backpacker accommodation, but luckily, he didn't have to share a room with anyone else. He went to bed early that first night, slept fitfully, and woke the next morning with a few important things to take care of: the first was to check that Omar had paid the balance of the money he owed, and the second was to find an apartment, then pay the deposit and upfront rent in cash which he'd already withdrawn. He could then open a bank account and after that, go to the registration offices of The Cordon Bleu, where he planned to enroll, and spend the next year learning how to cook both cuisine and pastry. He'd grown up eating bad Scottish food and on leaving the country, vowed that he'd eat better food for the rest of his life, especially when he had to make it himself. The course would cost more than twice what most people earn in a year, but Walter was now a wealthy man, and besides, money wasn't the point. He just wanted to know how to make good food. How wonderful would that be?

He phoned his new bank in Zurich – the account set up with the help of Omar- and having gone through security questions, was advised that a deposit of the amount Walter expected had been made. Well done, Omar. He would have known soon after Walter had done his job that Weber was dead. Walter didn't know how he'd found out, and he didn't care to know how but it was no surprise. Omar had sources of information all over the place, some of them, no doubt, inside Weber's bank.

Having got the duller, more administrative, side of things out of the way, he went along to "chef school" as he called it. Enrolling was a little trickier than he thought. Even international students needed to speak French at a basic level, so before entering, he'd need to embark on an intense six- month language course. The school's reception and admissions people were fabulous and had kindly tested Walter's language skills with some casual conversation: they estimated that six months of study should be fine. They also explained exactly what French language diploma he'd require and where he could take the course. With nothing else to do there, he left chef school, went to the language school, and signed up for a course. He also made the registration payment, then got on with his life.

The best way to get to know a city is by walking the streets. So, every morning, he'd get up, wash, and then walk until dusk. After a week of doing this and weighing up the costs, the access to Moroccan food, the walking distance to chef school, and an element of anonymity, he plumped for one of the districts not too far from the Eiffel Tower as the area he'd like to live in. He could walk to chef school in thirty minutes which would give him some extra exercise every day.

Chef school was choc-a-bloc with foreign students. Prudence would have loved the school, he thought.

He found a fabulous little one bedroom apartment with a separate bathroom and a kitchen unit with fridge, cooker and kettle inside the living room. The flat was on the second floor of the building and looked out across the street- a busy little street with a range of shops selling toys, electrical goods, coffee, holidays and property, and while the flat was run down, it was clean and it suited Walter down to the ground. It was bright. The difference between this and the dark, damp flat he grew up in was like night and day. There was a mini market not too far away and bars and cafés nearby that he could visit during the days or evenings when it suited him. He was feeling sorted, at least for the time being.

He wondered who he would cook for when he became an accomplished chef, but that wasn't the point he told himself. The skills he wanted to learn were for him, not anyone else. When out with the French soldiers in Marrakech they'd always joked about how bad British food was, as most other nations do, and Walter, in one of the few conversations they had, went to great lengths to describe the horrific food he'd eaten growing up, all of it deep fried, much of it burned or undercooked. There never seemed to be a happy medium. When he was a boy and cooked for himself, it was fried eggs only, the heat turned up so high that the whites frothed in the hot oil to ensure they weren't undercooked. He'd suffered from food poisoning a few times when growing up, and then overreacted, believing that only burnt food was one hundred percent safe. On the very rare occasion he had the money to eat out, he would do so, but it wouldn't be eating out in the traditional sense of the word- it was fish and chips or sausage and chips from a takeaway. A fish supper always seemed like a great idea at the time, and a real treat, and as he waited in line at the local chip shop listening to the husband and his wife, the two owners, berating each other in Italian, his mouth would water. Three bites in and he would start to feel queasy. He'd feel the food lying in his stomach for days, like Plaster of Paris, and eventually the feeling would disappear only to be replaced with the desire for another fish supper. Perhaps it was like taking drugs, thought Walter, and on balance he wasn't sure which of the two were the more likely to be fatal.

After starting at the language school, he quickly noticed that the Italian and French students fared much better than he did. They learned much faster. That said, Walter couldn't really understand why Italian and Spanish speaking people were at the class at all because, according to one Italian man about the same age as Walter, the grammar and vocabularies were very similar. English, however, was not, as Walter found out.

The class started at 9am every day, and finished at 3pm, with an hour off for lunch. The course was an immersion one which meant that no English, Spanish, Italian, Chinese, Korean- whatever- was to be spoken: only French.

On the first day during the morning coffee break, two groups formed in the canteen. The first group was the non-English speaking Europeans who managed to cobble together conversations using their own languages. And then there was the group that Walter was in, with one Chinese and one Korean student, and himself. The three of them stood in a corner smiling at each other, sipping espresso, unable to communicate. It suited Walter down to a T.

The homework he received each day was supposed to take twenty minutes to complete, but while he could speak a little of the language, he could write very little, and his understanding of grammar was well below a basic level. For the first month, the homework took him an hour or so, depending on the volume of it. As time went by though, despite the lessons becoming more advanced, Walter found himself improving, and the homework being less challenging. He was catching up. One of the tutors encouraged the students to get bar jobs if they had time, because it'd force them to talk to "real people" and advance the speed of their learning. Bar work wasn't the kind of thing that appealed to Walter because he liked to keep to himself, and he didn't need the money, but he understood the logic of the idea.

The tutor handed out the names of several bars that were open to language students, so Walter decided to go out that evening and have a look and see if he felt like applying for a job at any of them.

It was February now, and bitterly cold. After a third dinner in a row comprising salami and hard-boiled eggs- he needed to get out and shop properly- he wrapped up warmly in hiking boots, a long black coat and a short dark blue wool scarf wrapped tightly around his neck. His hair had grown much longer now and was curling at the back and the sides, and he could feel it lift like wings as he walked down his street against the evening wind. Snow fell gently, and as it began to lie, the sound of his footsteps faded to a muffled squeak, and he licked snowflakes from around his lips, opening his mouth sometimes and letting them fall directly onto his tongue, just as he had done when he was little.

The atmosphere in the first three bars was poor; they were very quiet, like Jacob's bar in Zurich, and so he decided they weren't for him because he didn't want to end up deep in conversation with anyone. He needed somewhere that was bustling, where there would be quick-fire conversation, nothing long enough to become overly personal. The fourth place he visited, Bar Pic, hit the spot.

It was busy, and after a short wait, he managed to catch the eye of what looked like the boss, behind the bar. He had short greying hair, a large stomach and well-tanned skin. He moved around behind the bar with confidence, talking with most of the customers and barking orders at bar staff. This wasn't a trendy bar; it was just a bar, and what caught Walter's attention were two painters or decorators, he guessed, still in overalls, deep in friendly conversation with two well-dressed businessmen in suits. Walter wondered what they were discussing. Two men and two women close to Walter's age stood close by, and this group too was deep in conversation. It seemed to be a bar for everyone, and Walter liked the ambience of the place. The music wasn't loud; it was just there doing its job of softening the tone. He hated bars where the music was so loud that he couldn't hear himself think. He liked music; he didn't like being deafened.

Once the patron had ambled over to him, Walter asked the man, in his prepared two sentences, what he wanted to ask- if there was a chance of a part time evening job, and that he'd been sent by his language school. The patron shrugged his shoulders and whistled in the direction of a young woman behind the bar who walked to Walter and said something he didn't understand. Walter repeated his questions. She answered in English as he expected. It was, no doubt, why she'd been asked to speak with him. She asked his name and they chatted for a while. She was nice. She'd discuss it with the patron after the shift, she said, and he should come back on Wednesday evening when she'd next be working to find out if there was a job for him or not. She suggested he have a drink and just watch for a while before leaving, and asked if he wanted a beer; but he declined and asked for a glass of red wine. She shrugged her shoulders, just like the patron had done earlier, then fetched a glass of wine for him. He thanked her and sat at the bar, watching.

It was warm inside, so he removed his coat and scarf and settled in. He did more watching of the barmaid he'd just spoken with than anything else, and he realised he hadn't introduced himself. When he ordered a refill, he told her he was named Walter, and asked her for her name. She was called Helen. No "e" at the end; and named after Helen of Troy. Her mother was a very dramatic person, she said.

"We both have old people's names." said Helen, then walked away.

On returning to Bar Pic on Wednesday evening, it turned out that there was a job for him cleaning tables, washing glasses, and serving behind the bar five nights per week. He started the next day, Thursday, and he enjoyed it. He was busy. The other bar staff knew the routine with language school interns, and so they were quite patient in helping Walter settle in. The patron spoke to Walter when he needed to, but he seemed to have absolutely no interest in him at all. He'd only bark orders, telling Walter to collect glasses, or change a beer barrel, or change bottles on a gantry, but that was all. Nothing personal.

At the end of each shift when the staff had managed to get the customers out, they sat at the bar to have a couple of drinks and enjoy some time to relax and unwind before heading to their homes. It was good, and Walter felt himself becoming a little bit more sociable as a person. Helen would often sit beside him, and he knew she'd do it on purpose. She was friendly, he thought, and pretty, and he wondered what kind of perfume she wore. It smelled nice. Whenever she turned to say something to someone else her hair swung round, almost brushing Walter's face and that was when he'd catch the scent of it. As she spoke to one of the other bartenders, he studied her and wondered to himself how he might describe her if asked to. She wasn't beautiful in traditional terms, but she was very attractive, with her neatly cut long black hair, a wide mouth, brown eyes, and a big personality which bordered on arrogance.

One evening she asked Walter where he lived so he told her, asking her in turn where she lived. He didn't know the street that she told him, but on asking, learned that it was in the same area as his apartment, not too far from him. She suggested that they walk home together, and Walter agreed, keen to do so. She linked arms with him against the cold. Helen was carrying an unwrapped bottle of brandy which she'd stolen from the bar. Thief. Without any suggestion from

Walter or encouragement from Helen- it just happened as if previously planned- they went up to Walter's apartment where he turned on the heating and lit some candles to add some warmth to the austerity of his place. He'd painted it all white, so it was fresh looking, and everything had been scrubbed clean; the floors, countertops, and the bed neatly made, but nothing hung on the walls. It looked like the room he'd occupied while in the army.

"Wow" said Helen. "Very tidy. It doesn't say much about you Walter, except that you're neat and clean. But that's good. Or maybe it says a lot." She laughed and rubbed his hair. "You've gone red in the face. Don't be angry, I'm only teasing."

Walter collected two glasses from a spotless wooden shelf in the kitchen, opened the brandy and poured large measures for them both. They sat on opposite sides of the small square wooden dining table that was placed in the middle of the rapidly heating room, and they both put their feet up, wondering what the other was thinking. Helen spoke Walter's language ten times more proficiently than Walter spoke Helen's, so they stuck to English. Walter wasn't bothered about how well he progressed language wise, as long as he made it into chef school. His mission was learning how to cook, not learning how to tell people his life story in French. Having taken off their boots outside his front door Walter noticed that Helen was wearing two odd woollen socks- one red and one black- which he told her said a lot about her. She laughed at that, and two brandies later, they made their way to Walter's tidy bed.

As the days and nights progressed, Walter enjoyed Helen's company more and more, and looked forward to the days he was on duty, because following work, she'd come home with him. On the days he wasn't working, he tended to stay in watching television programmes he couldn't really understand, just for study. The longer his relationship with Helen went on, the more comfortable he became with her, agreeing on occasion to stay at her apartment which, unlike his, was shared, and with two women that Walter didn't particularly like. They seemed to be aloof, and if he was right, they spoke exceedingly quickly so that he couldn't understand a word they said. Not very friendly. Helen's room was untidy which drove Walter mad. There were always stained cups or glasses lying around, unwashed clothes on the floor, and he could hardly see out of the window because it was so dirty. He much preferred it when she visited him. Despite her living differently to the way Walter did, he never judged her, because there was nothing to judge in his view. He liked her company, loved her sense of humour. That was more than enough, he thought.

One evening, they lay back in his bed, the room warm, both of them chilling happily. Walter had both hands under his head supporting it, enjoying the moment of tranquility in Helen's company. She was finishing off the cigarette they'd just shared, and she turned to stub it out on the ashtray that lay on his chest.

"What on earth are those marks on your armpits?" she asked. Walter moved the ashtray out of the way.

"Nothing."

"Let me see."

"I don't want to talk about it."

For close to ninety minutes this went on, back and forth, her asking him to explain and him refusing. They drank more and eventually Walter relented and told the story of how when he was a child, he'd told his mother about the dreams that terrified him. He had sought her help and comfort. She responded by putting out cigarettes in his armpits on various occasions over a period of months, to toughen him up, she said. He never asked her anything again. Helen never asked Walter anything personal again.

One Saturday, with no language school classes to attend, and Walter not working a shift at Bar Pic, he decided to go out and buy Helen a present; just something small to show that he cared, and he liked her. He bought a large candle for her room, infused with a vanilla scent. He didn't plan to go to the bar to meet her after work because they didn't do that- they only went home together after working together, and that suited Walter because he didn't want to rush things. That said, he thought the candle would be a nice gift, showing that she wasn't taken for granted. He'd give it to her when she next came round to his apartment, most likely the following evening.

She came home with him after work the following evening as expected and when he went to pour their drinks, he picked up the carefully wrapped present on the countertop then gave it to her.

She looked at it and asked him what it was. He told her it was a small gift. Helen didn't unwrap it, but instead handed it back to a confused Walter.

"Don't you want to open it?"

"No. I don't want your presents. I don't want you getting attached to me."

She stood up and went to the door, putting her boots on.

"I don't understand," said Walter, "what's wrong? It's just a small gift."

"Walter, you're just someone to sleep with. Nothing else. I hate it when guys get too close. It's creepy. The minute someone buys me something, it's the end. I don't want anything more to do with you. I'll choose who I want to get close to, not the other way round."

Walter watched in silence as she finished putting her boots on, followed by her coat.

"We can still be friends Walter. I don't dislike you. See you at Bar Pic tomorrow night."

She turned and left.

Walter sat with his brandy, saddened and confused by what had just happened. He didn't know whether to hate her or hate himself, or if he should be hating anyone at all for that matter. He didn't understand what he'd done wrong despite Helen's explanation, and the thought of facing her the next night at Bar Pic was unpleasant because he didn't know how he'd react when he saw her. Was he supposed to just laugh it off, pretend it hadn't happened? Apologise? How was he supposed to act? He felt like a fool, both for not understanding, and for opening up to her the way he had. It took him until around 3am to settle on the idea that just because she didn't react the way he would have if she'd bought him a gift, it didn't mean she was wrong. Perhaps. Having spent hours coming to that conclusion he changed his mind immediately. What was he thinking? She was horrible. It was really quite simple. He'd keep working at Bar Pic, literally pretend nothing had happened, and get what he needed from the job as intended.

Most of the following day, Walter couldn't focus at the language school. He couldn't work out if he was overly sensitive or not, stupid perhaps, and if anyone else would have just brushed it off. What didn't he know? That was the whole problem: his experiences in life seemed to have completely detached him from understanding how everyone else lived and conducted themselves.

He went to work that evening, and when the shift finished and everyone sat around the bar talking, Helen turned to Walter and told him that he shouldn't worry- she'd never tell anyone about his armpits. Walter looked at her steadily. Why would she think she needed to say that? It was the equivalent of saying, "Hey don't worry; I won't pour boiling fat over you." He downed his drink and walked out, never returning to Bar Pic.

He continued at language school, studying diligently, returning to his apartment in the late afternoons and studying more in the evenings, often going out too, enjoying the city as spring arrived.

He bumped into Helen one warm May evening as he was out walking. She stopped in front of him, blocking his path but he said nothing because he didn't know what to say. He was still deeply embarrassed about opening up to her then being so bluntly rejected. Worse, he didn't really know if he was justified in feeling like that or if he was just weak. As Helen stood there, he would have happily just sunk into the ground if he could. She peppered him with questions, asking why he hadn't returned to work; was he still living in the same apartment; did he have a new girlfriend- it didn't seem to stop. She spoke to him as if they were the best of friends, yet Walter didn't understand why she was talking to him at all, or what she wanted. So, he said nothing. He moved past her politely and kept walking, even as she called after him.

Chapter 18. Summer Heat, Paris, June 1977.

Walter sat his language exam at The Cordon Bleu which turned out to be much easier than he thought. The language course had stood him in good stead. He was enrolled to start chef school as he still called it (that would need to change) at the end of summer. Right now, he had a baking hot summer in Paris to look forward to. Language school was finished, bar work was finished. He'd enjoy himself.

The best way to combat the stifling heat during the day would be on a scooter, he thought, and at night in bed, with a super-powerful fan for his bedroom. The living room was usually cool because a nice breeze filtered through when he opened the windows. Walter bought both a fan and a scooter. The scooter was silver, an Italian imported Vespa with a top speed of sixty kilometres per hour. That made it absolutely perfect for busy Parisian traffic, hot French sun and thousands of tourists. He was able to stay out of the busy touristy areas and explore the real city. He still tended to stick to the city, rarely venturing out to the suburbs because they were less interesting and often lacked beauty and happiness. Many of them contained ugly modern housing blocks, sad estates with drugs, poverty and prostitution, just like much his home country. It felt like returning home, only hotter, so he stayed away.

From time to time, he engaged in forward planning as he thought about chef school. As his culinary skills would develop over time, he wanted to be able to practise them at his own apartment despite the limited space and equipment. If he was going to do that, he'd need to know where to buy the best fish, meat, vegetables, coffee, flour, and wine. Also, butter, milk, spices, herbs, jams, accoutrements.

He changed his exercise routine in an effort to stay super fit, rising early each morning to run through the quiet streets for mile after mile, returning to his apartment when they became busier.

Inside his apartment he practised the skills he'd learned in the army. While they'd never leave him now, if he didn't keep working out, he'd get slow. His days were busy and productive.

Over the weeks he built an extensive list of shops and markets where he could find everything he felt he'd want when he learned how to cook, and he kept detailed notes in a book with square lined pages that he'd bought especially for the purpose.

Just after six pm one evening, as the city started to cool, the phone in his apartment rang. This was odd, because the only people who knew his number were Helen, (and he hoped it wasn't her calling) the chef school, the language school, and his bank: as far as he could remember, that was it. He picked it up.

"Hello."

"Walter, my boy," said a jovial-sounding Omar.

This wasn't a welcome call.

"How did you get my number?"

"It's not hard," said Omar. "How are you?"

"What can I do for you, Omar?"

"You're a rich man, Walter. Are you enjoying life?"

"I am, thank you Omar." Walter didn't dislike Omar; he just wasn't the kind of person you wanted in your life.

"Would you like to get even wealthier?" So that was it. Walter had suspected for some time that a call like this might come, so he was ready.

"No, thank you. I'm retired. I'm enjoying life."

"Life could be twice as enjoyable with twice the money. And this time there is someone even more truly terrible that doesn't deserve to be alive, Walter. He's from my part of the world where there are many beautiful people, but sadly there are some bad ones too. This man lives in Paris- what a coincidence- and he also works in the slave trade. He kidnaps girls and smuggles them over here to a network of wholly undesirable people on the continent. These girls are gone for good once they leave France. Never seen again."

"That's very sad Omar, he sounds even more truly terrible as you describe him, but why are you involved? Have you become a concerned citizen in your old age?"

"I'm always concerned about my city and my country, Walter. But to answer your question, this man is also involved in drugs, nightclubs and all sorts. He's upsetting my broader business family."

"You mean the same business family that Weber upset, is that correct?"

"Exactly. This man is named Ben."

"What's his surname, Omar?"

"It's Ben; his first name is Louis. He has some French blood mixed into his family history."

"Louis Ben isn't a problem that I want to sort, Omar. I'm sorry. I'm guessing that there is now an endless supply of similar people that you'll want me to deal with. The Weber assignment was justified and a means to an end for me. I don't want any more. You'll need to find someone else."

"Walter, an envelope is in your mailbox downstairs in your apartment building. Inside is a photograph and information about where you will find Ben. We can get you another weapon of your choice, whatever you need."

"The answer is no, Omar."

"Read what's in the envelope Walter. I'll call you this time tomorrow. Okay?"

"Okay, but the answer will be the same. And don't put anything else in my mailbox."

"Alright my friend, let's speak tomorrow."

"One thing, Omar, before you go." Walter tensed. "How is Prudence?" He tried to ask in an offhand manner and failed.

"She's fine, I'll tell her you said hello. I'll call tomorrow." Omar put the phone down.

"Fine" Omar had said of Prudence- that was all. Well, what did Walter expect him to say? "Oh, Walter, I'm so glad you asked, she can't live without you."

Truth be told, what kind of father would want their daughter in a relationship with someone like him anyway, he thought. Besides, if she'd been keen on talking to him, she'd have found a way. He told himself that he needed to get a grip of himself. He was thinking like a fool.

He decided to go for a walk and forget about her, but with each step he wondered who she was seeing now. He still couldn't understand why she hadn't met him at the café on the last day. It just didn't feel right. And yet, was it so hard to believe that she'd just grown bored of him, or had met someone in Marrakech and fallen for them?

On his return to his apartment building, he retrieved the envelope in his mailbox, and when upstairs again, studied the photographs and information about Louis Ben.

Well, there would never be any difficulty spotting Ben in the street, thought Walter. He looked like a caricature of the evil villain from any film that had an evil villain in it. Ben didn't worry Walter in the slightest though, and indeed, the idea of someone looking as Ben did, and being a villain, brought a smile to his face. Ben was bald, tall, and well-built with a nose that had obviously been broken many times. This didn't indicate that he was a tough guy, just that he'd had his nose broken. However, Walter didn't for a second underestimate how dangerous the man was. He was the leader of a sizeable, ruthless outfit, but none of it changed how Walter felt. He didn't need money and didn't want to do mercenary work, and he didn't want to create any trouble for himself. He only wanted to learn how to cook.

When Omar called the next evening Walter told him, politely, that he hadn't changed his mind, and as much as he appreciated the offer, he wouldn't work for Omar again.

"I understand, Walter." said Omar. "Perfectly. Now I will hang up and leave you in peace."

Omar was so polite that Walter almost felt guilty, but instantly recognised that to be a ridiculous feeling.

"Well, tell Prudence I was asking for her." He could have kicked himself for saying that. It sounded childish. He really wished Omar hadn't called. Walter tried to think of something to say straight after, in an attempt to sound more business-like but it didn't matter. Omar had already hung up.

Chapter 19. The Vespa, Paris, August 1977.

Walter spent the end of June and all of July reading, finding more shops to buy food at, running, and many evenings he'd be out and about exploring the city on his Vespa. He'd found a bar he particularly liked, close to the exquisite Notre Dame de Paris. Despite the proximity to the cathedral, the bar was off the tourist trail, so it suited Walter. Often, he'd pull his Vespa up outside the bar about ten pm and go inside to enjoy a glass or two of beer, having switched from wine for the hot summer months. He'd also found someone who would sell him something to smoke from time to time- a very pleasant, mild marijuana. One particularly hot evening, he decided to sit outside. As he relaxed at a small round table sipping his beer and looking around the street at the people passing by, a car drove past much more slowly than a car would normally do. Louis Ben was sitting in the passenger seat staring directly at Walter. His window was wound down and he was pointing a pistol at Walter. He fired just as Walter reacted and dived to the ground. The bullet flew past him, missing everyone around him, but it did shatter the glass front to the bar.

The car screeched off, and Walter, utterly incensed, stood, dusted himself off, walked to his scooter and sped home to call the man responsible for this: Omar.

Walter had quickly looked around the bar after the shooting and seen that no one was hurt, although everyone was understandably terrified. It was important that he get out of there quickly. The bar staff would be aware that he was a foreigner, but that was about it. They couldn't tell the police anything about him other than that. It was highly annoying though, because they'd have known he had a scooter too, so indeed they had some information about him. Not for the first time he found himself grateful that Paris was the most visited city in the world and a city full of scooters: he hoped he'd not be traced. He hadn't broken any laws, but once they knew about his background in the army, he'd be on the police radar, and his permit to stay in the country could be revoked.

He poured himself a brandy when he got back to his apartment, sat at the small table in his living room and called Omar. He wasn't at home, but a message was taken, and Walter was assured that Omar would return his call. No matter how hard he tried to think of ways this could have come about without Omar being the cause, he could think of none. There were none. His phone rang an hour later, and Walter picked it up.

He listened as Omar, flustered in a way that Walter had never heard him before, apologised, and explained. It was a mess of his own making.

Louis Ben had been told via third party sources- information fed to them by Omar himself- that a group of ambitious drug dealers, led by a young British man, Walter, were starting to get a foothold in Paris and would soon be encroaching on his territories and business both there and in north Africa.

Omar had done this in the hope that Ben would approach Walter to warn him off. Walter, on recognising Ben, would fear for his life and kill him.

"Why on earth would you do such an incredibly stupid thing and make up such a ridiculous and complicated story?" said Walter. "It doesn't make any sense at all. What have I ever done to you? It's nonsensical. What's more, I'd already told you I wasn't going to kill him for you. And instead of taking me at my word, you've created this ludicrous plan that could have seen me killed, just so that you could get your way. And now, I will need to kill him because that's exactly what he wants to do to me."

Walter paused before continuing.

"I will kill him Omar, but then I'm coming for you. I trusted you, but you let me down. I shouldn't be surprised; everyone lets me down. Especially in your family."

"I was desperate, Walter." Omar was weeping. "Ben has taken Prudence and is using her as a bargaining tool because he wants me to sell him my bars and nightclubs. When he first approached me about buying my business interests I refused, and then two weeks ago, they kidnapped her. A month or so back you told me in no uncertain terms that you wouldn't kill Ben. I had to act. I thought maybe he'd just threaten you; I didn't think he'd try to kill you, but I knew that you'd kill him if you saw him as a threat."

He didn't apologise, and Walter understood why. He'd do anything for his daughter.

"Where is Prudence- can you get her back? Surely, killing Ben will endanger Prudence even more?" Walter felt sick.

"If I can get Louis Ben killed then I will get Prudence back. Me and my friends- you know who- can work with his current subordinates. I know this to be true. We've already spoken. But right now, everyone in Ben's group is terrified of acting against him. No one will do it. If Ben is killed though, and is out of the picture, I can get Prudence back because his people will take over his business and work with me, not against me. Ben is the only problem. Killing Ben gets Prudence back alive. Walter, if you do this, I'll pay you twice what you were paid for Switzerland." Omar had spewed the words out at speed, his panic apparent.

"I don't want your money, Omar. Why didn't you just tell me what was going on?"

"I thought this way would be more certain– I wasn't sure that you'd get involved on behalf of Prudence. I just acted in panic."

"Well then you're an idiot and a poor judge of character. Why didn't you just have one of your people do it?"

"They're white-collar criminals Walter, they couldn't kill anyone themselves. They'd get killed in the process of trying."

Something was troubling Walter far more deeply than Omar's stupidity: for the first time in his adult life, Walter felt fear while awake, but not for himself; for Prudence. How illogical. This was the woman who had broken his heart. And now he feared for her life?

He explained to Omar what was going to happen.

"I will sort this out within forty- eight hours. Not for you and not for me."

"I know Walter- you will do it for Prudence. I knew you would."

"No, you didn't" corrected Walter. "You just told me you weren't sure if I would help or not. If you were sure, you'd have been honest with me and asked for my help earlier."

Omar said nothing: he was a broken man and would have said anything to have Walter help him. Walter left his statement hanging.

"You will tell no one that we have spoken, Omar. You have proven yourself stupid and unreliable. I will call you when things are sorted over here, then you will secure the immediate return of Prudence in good health. I want to hear her voice on the phone when you have her back. That will be proof of her safe return. So, let me make this completely clear for you Omar. If you do not call me, with Prudence by your side, within twenty-four hours of me sorting things here, I will know that you have either reneged or simply failed and if that is so I will come for you. Do you understand all of that?"

"I do, Walter, I'm sorry … I didn't know what else to…"

Walter was incensed by the stupidity and selfishness of Omar. He hung up.

Omar had trapped Walter in a situation he couldn't get out of. Even if he chose not to help Prudence, Ben would come for him. He had no choice but to act.

This was ugly, and against Walter's nature, but he had to proceed. He'd vowed to himself never to kill again, and yet months later, here he was, planning to do just that. He should never have agreed to kill Weber.

Having read everything that Omar had given him about Ben when he was first contacted a couple of months ago, Walter knew where to find him. Tomorrow morning at dawn, he'd get onto his Vespa, and go to deal with Ben, who would pay for what he'd done to Prudence.

As he lay awake in bed, he wrestled with every aspect of what he had been forced into doing. He hated Omar for this. The only positive coming out of it was that Prudence would be safe, and Walter would rid himself of Omar and his ugly friends for good. And then he would genuinely be free. The upcoming hours and days would bring closure to his days in Morocco.

Chapter 20. A Twist of fate. The following morning.

The sun wasn't up yet, but it soon would be. Walter felt the rush of cool morning air against his face as he sped along the embankment towards the café where Louis Ben went every morning for breakfast. Arrogant men view themselves as untouchable and Ben would never change his habits for the sake of some young up-and-coming drug dealer that he'd tried to kill the night before. It would be a sign of cowardice and that would not do.

The Vespa weaved in and out of the sparse early morning traffic that was building, and within twenty minutes of leaving his apartment, Walter was parked two blocks from where Ben would soon arrive to eat. From a discreet vantage point across the road where he blended in with some other early risers sitting peacefully looking over the Seine as the sun rose, Walter smoked and discretely kept an eye on the café. Over the next thirty minutes, lights went on, doors were opened, tables and chairs which had been chained together overnight were freed and wiped down. The café looked nice, and Walter regretted that he couldn't get a coffee and a bite to eat there himself.

At 6:30am the sun was up, and just as the briefing paper from Omar had stated, Louis Ben arrived for breakfast. He sunk his huge frame into a small chair outside and picked up the morning paper on his table.

Walter waited until Ben's breakfast had arrived and was taking up his attention. The waitress who'd served him had returned indoors, and at this early hour no one else sat outside. They soon would though, so Walter had to move quickly. Ben had put down the newspaper and moved his chair a little so that he was facing the rising sun as he ate, a lucky break for Walter, because it meant he had his eyes half closed while he ate, simultaneously soaking up the early heat like a lizard. He wasn't paying attention to his surroundings and was clearly not at all worried. So arrogant.

Walter left his spot at the river's edge, and making his way across the road, was able to approach Ben from behind, in complete silence. He wasn't aware of Walter's presence. In a single motion, Walter wrapped one arm around Ben's forehead and with the other held his chin. He twisted through one hundred and eighty degrees and back again with every ounce of strength he had. Ben's neck snapped loudly, confirming for Walter that what needed to be done, was done.

Walter walked away calmly, and made his way to his trusty Vespa. As he sped back to his apartment, he felt sick inside but continually told himself that he'd had no choice in the matter. No matter what, given the nature of Ben and the time pressure Walter was under to sort this out, he couldn't see any other way of resolving the situation. The simple truth was, he had had to do it to save his own life and Prudence's. It was a decision that he could live with. He would have to.

He rang Omar on his return to his apartment. The idiot sounded sleepy when he picked up the telephone.

"Done." was all Walter said, and he hung up.

That evening, he stayed by the telephone waiting for the call. It came around nine pm. The whole transaction had been done well within the time frame.

"Walter, it's Omar, thank you. I have made arrangements to pay you twice what I paid you for Switzerland. Say nothing. It's done. I owe you everything."

"I don't want your money. Did you get Prudence- is she safe?"

"Hold on."

"Walter, it's Prudence."

He said nothing, and seconds passed in silence as tears streamed down his lonely face. They had come out of the blue and he didn't know why. The fact was, he was feeling something he hadn't felt since he was a little boy. She had completely crushed him.

"Walter, that day- your last day here- I need to explain something."

He didn't want her to explain anything. More words meant more trouble. She was safe now, and he must move on. He hung up.

Five minutes passed, and he regretted hanging up- it was childish. He wanted to hear what she had to say, so he called back, but the line was now busy, and it stayed busy for hours, and then days, then weeks as he kept trying until he finally gave up.

That night and for a long time after he slept more poorly than he usually did, and the recurring dream was back with a vengeance.

He was never able to reach Prudence again, and just as it had happened in Morocco, she disappeared from his life and didn't contact him again.

Chapter 21. Chef School, Paris, September 1977.

Walter walked with a spring in his step for the first time in a month. The trauma of the incident with Louis Ben combined with the second time Prudence had vanished from his life was fading a little with each day that passed. He was now richer than he could ever have dreamt possible, having been surprised to see that Omar had indeed paid him twice what he had been paid for Zurich. He thought briefly about returning the money but decided that given the degree of Omar's stupidity, he was owed it. It was time to rebuild his life, permanently this time. He was changing, and for the first time in his life he was going to do something which wasn't a means to an end.

He stopped outside the building that housed the chef school and looked up at the facade. He could feel a sense of belonging. It wasn't rational, but it was there. He'd read a lot about the various courses, and the master chefs; and he saw them as artists, which was also how they saw themselves. He'd opted for the most intense and longest of the courses, the grand diploma, which would incorporate teaching of cuisine, pastry and confectionery, and wine. The course was nine months long, and while he'd been told that upon qualifying, he could pursue different careers, such as training to be a master chef, or becoming a food writer, Walter had no plans to do any such thing. He now had other plans.

The first day at the school was interesting. There were many other students; some French, some from overseas, including a couple of Brits who Walter made a mental note to stay away from, whenever possible. Everyone was nervous. Walter found it bizarre that he was much more intimidated by the chefs than he had been by some of the violent individuals, including terrorists, that he'd come up against during his time in the army. It was all new. Or perhaps it was because for the first time in his life, he really cared about succeeding.

As the weeks wore on, and the weather changed, it was fabulous to leave the cold air of the streets and enter the school in the mornings.

Some of the teachers were patient and kind, but the school wanted the pupils to excel, to push themselves to do great things, so there was also a lot of shouting, criticism and barking of orders. This kind of treatment was not new to Walter, so while tears flowed among some of the recruits, it was just fine with him. He worked hard, listened, and loved it.

Walter saw the course as his entry into the real world, so he started to make some effort to integrate with the other students, even the British ones he'd initially wanted to avoid. He wasn't completely averse to speaking with other British students, he just felt he'd left his homeland behind, emotionally as well as physically. On the surface, he had nothing to hide. He had been in the army, left with a good record and now wanted to pursue a different career. He just didn't want to talk about it with fellow Brits who might ask too many questions. That was his past, and he was now thinking of his future.

Whenever the students were given a break during the day, they made their way downstairs and stood outside the front of the building with a coffee in one hand and a cigarette in the other. Some of the students came from wealthy backgrounds. Some had managed to find sponsorship and were under great pressure to succeed. As Christmas approached, during one of the pastries and confectionery classes, Walter's favourite chef and teacher Vincent, or "Chef" as he was called during class, asked each of the students what they were going to do over the Christmas break. They were all either sitting or standing in the huge and magnificent warm kitchen- twenty students waiting while their bread rose in their assigned ovens. Vincent went round each student, one by one, asking what their plans were. Most of them, whether they were French, German, Italian, Chinese, British, Japanese, Korean, or Spanish, were heading home to be with family, though one or two of the Chinese and Japanese students were staying in France. Walter's turn came and he said that he'd be doing exactly as the majority were doing; going home. Vincent looked at Walter as he spoke and asked him where home was, to which Walter answered, Edinburgh.

"Are your parents there?"

"Yes," he replied.

Vincent was in his late forties. He was a highly skilled chef and a good human being who knew a lie when he heard it- but he said nothing.

Just as Vincent knew that Walter had lied, Walter knew that Vincent knew.

Vincent had bags under his blue eyes, a hooked Roman nose and greying hair, which was a little bit messy. It wouldn't have cut mustard in the army.

During his six years in the army, Walter had always volunteered to work through the festive period. Sometimes he wouldn't have had a choice even if he had wanted to return home, but his willingness to work over Christmas was always welcomed by the army. In Zurich, he'd spent Christmas day by himself, constructing and deconstructing the rifle but took time off to enjoy a few whiskies and wish himself a Merry Christmas. He wasn't oblivious to the fact that spending Christmas on his own was a sad state of affairs, but it was preferable to returning home. There was nothing for him there. He'd once seen a photograph of one of the four Scream paintings by Edvard Munch- the one on the bridge- and like many others had felt before him, it perfectly portrayed his feelings about his childhood home. So, having a few whiskies this year on his own in Paris, just as he'd done in Zurich the year before was immeasurably better than a trip home.

At the end of the day, as he stood in the busy cloakroom and wrapped his blue wool scarf around his neck and reached for his long coat, Walter was tapped on the shoulder. He turned to see Vincent who asked him to follow him. Walter did as he was asked, following him into the kitchen which was now empty. Vincent looked into Walter's eyes and asked him if he'd please join him and his wife, and various other waifs, at his home for Christmas dinner. Walter smiled, not in the least surprised by this generous offer, and so he accepted. It was in ten days' time. Vincent handed Walter a piece of paper with the time and address written on it. He added that Walter needn't bring anything with him.

"Thank you, Chef. I'll be there."

"Good. See you then."

In the days leading up to Christmas, the classes focused on pastry and bread, and Walter found himself as happy as he'd ever been, having mastered the art of preparing and baking exquisite croissants and baguettes. As the Chef explained to the pupils, making a croissant is easy. Making a good croissant is difficult. Making a great croissant is art, and unless you're an artist, you will never be able to make a great croissant.

Walter was becoming an artist. Both his baguettes and his croissants were superb, roundly applauded by his teachers. Making them gave Walter as much joy as anything he'd done before. He'd look into the school's ovens and open them, smelling the croissants as they baked- something he wasn't actually supposed to do. On removing the finished croissants from the ovens, his mouth would water as they cooled, and he'd inspect them closely to ensure that they were the perfect colour. Then came the tasting, which was of course the part he enjoyed most. The process of pulling them apart and then listening for the light crunch as he bit into them then chewed; it was a unique experience. They went beautifully with coffee and hot chocolate in his view. The phrase "the simple pleasures in life" now had meaning for Walter.

The end of term came, and using knowledge he'd learned at school, Walter went to one of the wine stores he'd found during the days he spent scouring the city for good food and wine resources. He bought two good bottles of red wine and a box of chocolates that he felt both Vincent and his wife would enjoy. Naturally, he'd ignored instructions not to bring anything.

Chapter 22. Prudence. Quebec. September 1977.

She sat alone in a diner in Rue Du Cul De Sac, having breakfast. Everything she owned in her now harsh and lonely world was in a small rucksack on the floor beside her.

Later in the day she planned to visit the immigration authorities and see if there was any way she could find out where Walter Mack had gone after his arrival. It was likely that they wouldn't tell her anything, and if so, she'd try some other way of tracking him down, but she wasn't quite sure what that could be. It seemed as if she had an almost impossible task ahead of her.

Added to that, she wasn't wholly convinced that Walter was in Quebec, or indeed, even in Canada. Her father had said that he didn't want her trying to find Walter and so his telling her that he was here was possibly a calculated ploy– a lie- to put her off. Canada being mostly an English speaking country though, combined with the language link to Morocco made sense, however, and made Prudence think it might just be true. All good lies had a hint of truth in them which is why they're good lies. But she was five thousand two hundred and seventy kilometres from Walter.

Chapter 23. Christmas Day, Paris 1977.

Walter Mack arrived at a street named Rue des Barres in the fourth district of the city and found the building he was looking for. Looking around before ringing the buzzer, he saw a picture-perfect street setting for Christmas. It was like a postcard. He wondered who the other "waifs" attending the dinner were. He rang the door buzzer.

Vincent greeted him and gave him a hearty welcome, taking his coat and scarf, as well as the nicely wrapped wine and chocolates. His wife, Veronique, came out to greet him too. She was beautiful- certainly old enough to be Walter's mother, he thought, but not just beautiful; she was elegant, and warm. He felt guilty about being attracted to her.

He was led into a large living room with rugs on polished wooden floors, and an open fire of burning logs. On top of the mantelpiece were dozens of Christmas cards. It reminded Walter that he'd never received a Christmas card before. A Christmas tree stood in the corner. The room was sparsely decorated, apart from the tree, but very tastefully done. He admired the style. It was beautiful. Being late afternoon now, the living room's lamps were on, the candles lit and the fire giving the room a luscious glow.

"Am I the first?" asked Walter, noticing that he appeared to be the only guest, unless others were in other rooms.

"There's no one else coming, Walter." said Veronique. "You wouldn't have agreed to come if Vincent had said it would just be you. So, I asked him to tell a tiny lie." She smiled at Walter, using her forefinger and thumb to emphasise the "tiny" point.

"How did you know that I'd be on my own when you asked the class what they'd be doing over Christmas?" asked Walter, looking at Vincent.

"I guessed," he said. "But it's not charity, Walter. I like you, and Veronique and I like good company on Christmas day."

He'd be the focus of attention today, but Walter knew he was in good company. Good people. This would be a nice Christmas day.

He relaxed more than he'd done in a long time, especially after some champagne and wine. The food was superb, of course: inspirational in fact, and Walter ate everything he was offered. Both Veronique and Vincent asked him about himself, but they didn't probe even when they noted large swathes of his life remaining unaccounted for. They were impressed that he'd been in the army and that he enjoyed Moroccan food so much. When Veronique asked about Walter's love life, he became quiet and evasive, so again they didn't probe. Walter asked what Veronique did for a living, and she told him that she was a psychologist. He was interested in hearing what it was that she did on a day-to-day basis.

Veronique talked for a while about the kind of help her patients tended to need and the processes she went through with them.

"The biggest challenge I have is that people feel embarrassed admitting that they need help at all, or else they're embarrassed about the problem they have that they need to talk through. In men, especially, they think that it's a sign of weakness."

Walter responded, "I don't mean to sound rude, though this probably will sound just that, but does what you do always work?"

Veronique raised her eyebrows and shrugged her shoulders.

"Often it does, it's not an exact science. There are people who can't be helped, or deep down don't want to be helped. The mind is a very complicated thing. It works best for those who really want to be helped. Are you interested in treatment, Walter?"

He laughed, and said he was just fine as he thought about his recurring dream- but he thanked her for the offer.

"Well, anytime you feel like talking, we can do it in complete confidence."

Walter thanked her again but declined with a polite hand gesture. He was interested though. He'd do anything to wipe the recurring dream from his tormented soul.

The rest of the evening was also superb, and sitting in a warm, beautiful apartment in a beautiful street in a beautiful city with beautiful people, Walter soaked it all up. It was the best Christmas he'd ever had.

Chapter 24. Prudence. Quebec. That same Christmas Day, 1977.

After three months looking around Quebec without any real plan, apart from going from bar to bar, and feeling early on that she had a hopeless task ahead of her, Prudence became despondent. She had no one to go to for help.

The authorities at immigration became suspicious when she had approached them, and they quickly turned their attention to her instead, asking how long she was staying, who was this Walter Mack and why was she looking for him? She hastily excused herself from the official she had managed to get a meeting with, saying she had to visit the bathroom and instead left the building.

She spent time wandering from district to district but as each day went by, the more foolish she felt.

She eventually called home on this Christmas day, hoping to speak with Tarik, her old bodyguard, but instead only managed to speak with the housekeeper, Martha. Tarik was gone– to Paris she'd heard. And her father was gone too– but he was dead. Omar had collapsed. Something to do with a blood clot to the brain. Her home was now occupied by people she'd never heard of, but she knew the type. Crooks. Her father's businesses would have been taken over along with the house and the money. That was the criminal underbelly of Marrakech for you. One day you're as rich as Croesus and the next day you're poorer than a dormouse. Or dead. Title deeds had little to do with anything. Money and intimidation were the most valuable currency. As much as she'd hated her father for what he'd done she suddenly felt desperately sad and alone and could only remember the good things about him. Like most bad people, some goodness could be found inside them even if buried deep, and she knew that as misguided as he'd been, he'd have done anything for her. She instantly regretted leaving Marrakech, as much as the fact that she now had nothing to go back to.

She was alone, and so her confidence all but vanished. Usually up for anything, she felt like curling into a ball and hiding under a table.

The only good news she heard from Martha was that Tarik had said he thought Walter was in Europe, perhaps Malaga in Spain, where Omar had– or used to have– several bars and nightclubs. Tired of Quebec, despondent, lonely, and miserable, she'd boarded a flight to Spain the next day.

Chapter 25. Unusual Friends. Paris, Spring 1978.

Classes at chef school recommenced in early January, and Walter immersed himself in all of it, loving every minute, even the occasions he was berated by one chef or another for his mistakes. Any time he failed at something, he improved shortly thereafter. His skills were improving quickly.

His understanding of wine improved too, and he learned that while he had good taste, much of what he was learning felt like a conspiracy by the wine producers that allowed them to charge as much as they wanted even though all wines were made from the same thing. That said, he had to admit, it did seem that the most expensive wines were indeed the best. So perhaps he was completely wrong in his thinking. He shouldn't be so quick to judge.

When it came to cuisine, he was good, and although he mastered the techniques used and required across all areas, it was pastry and confectionery that interested him the most.

On a late January morning as he stood outside during the cigarette break with the other students, and plumes of smoke and warm breath escaped from everyone, they talked about what they'd do after the course was finished. Everyone, with one exception, Walter, dreamed of having their own restaurant one day- after further training in a top- class restaurant either in Paris or in their hometown. Walter said that this is what he wanted to do too, but that was only to avoid any other talk about him or his plans.

Over the following months, one evening per week, around nine pm, Walter would meet Veronique and Vincent for a drink somewhere in the city, usually within walking distance of their apartment. They'd spend an hour or two talking about life, food, politics, and people, just like everyone else did in the bars they choose to meet at, and they'd share cigarettes and stories.

In late March, sitting inside a lively brasserie one evening, Vincent asked Walter what he'd do when the course was finished. Walter answered truthfully saying that he would at some point leave Paris. He just wasn't sure when. He liked the city, and he liked them.

"Don't you want to work, learn, improve?" asked Vincent.

"Yes, but I'm not sure that working in a restaurant is for me. I prefer the simpler things, maybe that's why I like making bread so much."

"You already make bread as well as anyone I know. I can help you find a job in a restaurant here in Paris if you'd like."

"You've already done so much for me, so I'll say a polite no. But thank you. I might do what you suggest though, and find a job, so I can hone my skills further, but I'll look for a job by myself."

"Why would you do that when I can find a job for you with one phone call?"

He was right, thought Walter. Why indeed? He nodded a polite thank you.
"Leave it with me; I think I know a good place," said Vincent.

"When someone offers you help, take it Walter," added Veronique.

Walter respected Vincent more now than anyone else he knew. There were a few people he'd met during his army days, such as Colonel McLellan, who he admired in some ways, but Vincent, through his skill and his kindness had earned Walter's utmost respect, as had Veronique, although he still didn't understand as much about her role as a psychologist as he did of Vincent's as a teacher of art.

The following week, at the same time, Walter turned up at a very simple bar, owned by a friend of Veronique. The patron was an old lady who looked older than the wood that most of the interior had been built with. Like everyone else in France, she smoked, so making his way through a blue haze, Walter reached the table where Veronique sat.

"I'm sorry I'm late," he said, "I took a couple of wrong turns getting here."

"Can I get you a drink?" he asked, about to go to the bar.

"I have one, thank you." she replied.

"Where's Vincent?" asked Walter. He hadn't seen him at chef school that day, but until now, thought nothing of it. He often went days at a time without seeing Vincent.

"He's in Lyon, as a guest chef for a friend of his who has a superb little bistro there. Sometimes Vincent asks him to come to Paris to talk at the school. You might meet him some day."

"Interesting," said Walter. "I'll be back in a second," and off he went to the bar to get a drink for himself, alarm bells ringing very loudly in his ears. Was it odd to be alone with Veronique, or was this normal?

He returned to the table and joined her. He had to admit, she looked stunning. He reminded himself that she was old enough to be his mother. Her dark hair was in a severe ponytail, which revealed large gold hoop earrings and a make-up free face, save for an extravagantly bright red lipstick.

Walter found her alluring and instantly hated himself for thinking this way. He felt terrible for lusting after Vincent's wife. There was something in the bible about the gravity of the sin of lusting after another man's wife; he was sure he'd read that. Vincent was a man who could now be classified as his best friend and his mentor. Walter mentally slapped himself across the face in a bid to sort himself out.

"Vincent knows we're meeting tonight," said Veronique, reading his mind, "he said to say hello and he'll see you at the school next week."

"Fabulous. When's he back?"

"At the weekend."

"To us then," toasted Walter and held up his glass, desperate to give the impression that all was fine inside his head.

The more they talked, the more engrossed he became with Veronique. Whichever the fragrance was that she wore, he loved it. When she insisted on going up to the bar for more drinks, despite his protestations, he watched and admired the way she carried herself. He studied her figure as she stood with her back to him, ordering, and his admiration for her grew in equal measure to his shame. Veronique looked over her shoulder at him and caught him looking- and at that point he knew that she knew what he was thinking. She smiled at him.

Rain beating against the shutters in Veronique's bedroom woke him the next morning. The shutters opened onto a small balcony with a small table and two small, ornate cast iron chairs that stayed out there all year round. The rust indicated this.

"I am truly the world's most horrible person" thought Walter keeping his eyes closed. "I have actually stabbed the only man I think I care about right between the shoulder blades."

He turned to talk to Veronique, but the bed was empty. As he looked around the empty bedroom, he could make out muffled voices from somewhere inside the house and could tell that

Veronique was on the phone somewhere else in the apartment. Perhaps that's what had woken him up, not the rain.

The bed was warm, and a thousand times more comfortable than the thing he slept in at his apartment. Fabulous pillows. His own pillows were hard and uncomfortable. He must change them.

The bedroom door opened, and Veronique came in, casually dressed in jeans and a faded blue tee shirt that had once been dark blue. She had a coffee in her hand for Walter which she handed to him and then sat on the edge of the bed beside him and kissed him on the cheek.

"Good morning, Walter."

"Morning." he smiled back, blushing.

She put her hand gently on his leg. "That was Vincent on the phone. He asked me to say hello."

Chapter 26. The Final Term. Paris. Spring 1978.

The morning after he'd slept with Veronique had been a baptism by fire for Walter in terms of understanding the many curious ways of love and affection. Prior to that, he'd believed himself to be quite worldly: he'd left home at fifteen, eaten scraps, travelled south, done odd jobs, joined the army and now attended chef school. But he was beginning to understand that the more experience he gained with the people of the world, the less he understood about them. Until now, his entire life had had some form of violence or nastiness at its core, but he was beginning to experience the complete opposite. It was an intoxicating and most welcome addition, though confusing at times, and definitely surprising.

At that particular moment in time though, the morning after he'd slept with Veronique, things were a little fraught. After spending ten minutes calming Walter down, Veronique had brought him another coffee and returned to her place at the edge of the bed.

"How can he not mind?" Walter asked.

"He likes you."

"So, he knew that this would happen, then, before we even met for a drink?"

"We both did, Walter. Vincent is a wonderful, insightful and secure man. We could both tell that you like me, just as you like Vincent, but in another way. Sometimes he will sleep with other women, and as long as I know who they are, and if I have said it's okay, then I am happy for him to do it."

"So, he doesn't think badly of me then?"

"No, he likes you."

Walter was wondering if he should feel guilty or stupid. Naive perhaps? Had he been managed- set up? It felt like it, but did it matter?

"Don't feel as if you've been set up," said Veronique. Walter was now convinced she could read his thoughts.

"The choice was always going to be yours. If you'd decided not to come back with me, that would have been fine too, but not as much fun."

She poked him in the ribs, and he jerked away from her, spilling coffee on the beautiful white sheets.

"I suppose, if you put it that way." He poked her back.

The following week, on the Monday, he saw Vincent at chef school, and having rehearsed this moment many times, under the tutelage of Veronique, he said, "Good morning," and shook his hand. Vincent clapped him on the back, saying "Good morning" then went on to teach his next class.

Having made it clear to Veronique that his liking of Vincent didn't go as far as the bedroom, he was now relaxed and looking forward to seeing both of them for a drink on the Thursday of that week.

Another bar which was new to Walter was chosen, and given the milder evening air, they sat outside drinking and enjoying the beautiful changing skies as the sun set. The bar was not only close to Veronique and Vincent's apartment but only twenty minutes' walk from Walter's apartment. He walked them home. They turned onto Rue de Barres- a busy street during the day due to tourists, but tonight the air had cooled quickly, and the sun had set, meaning it was now dark and empty.

Voices were raised behind them. Muggers.

Two young men, both with stiletto knives were walking towards them. Both men looked well fed and strong, and Walter wondered why they would need to mug anyone. It didn't look like they needed drug money, or money for food.

He looked over to Vincent who was calm but looking understandably concerned. Veronique was not calm at all, and was shouting at the two men, speaking so quickly that Walter didn't know what she was saying. Things had escalated very quickly indeed.

Vincent tried to pacify Veronique, but as he did, she ran at the approaching men intent on attacking them. This was madness; they were both armed. She threw a punch which missed by a mile as Vincent caught up with her and pulled her back. But the man she'd thrown the punch at slashed her arm cutting her, and she yelped.

Walter walked over to the man, holding his hands in the air and feigning surrender but instead stamped on the man's knee, who then collapsed. His friend lunged at Walter who dodged the blow and punched him, knocking him out. Walter turned to Vincent and Veronique, telling them to follow him right away. They left the two men and walked quickly, Walter in front, first turning one corner and then the next with a view to eventually doubleback to Rue des Barres shortly after. Walter planned to take the diversion to make sure that the two men didn't see where Vincent and Veronique lived.

Veronique stopped and turned to face Walter. "Let's go back Walter. I really want to kill them."

"Don't worry about them. You're safe." He replied. "Hold onto Vincent. Keep going."

"I'm serious, I want to go back and kill them." she shouted in his face.

Vincent had his arms wrapped around his wife, desperately trying to calm her but she wouldn't stop.

Walter joined Vincent in trying to calm her down and they both spent the next fifteen minutes talking to her until she eventually settled.
Walter told them to stay where they were and returned to the scene of the attempted mugging just in time to see the two men being loaded into the back of an ambulance. The doors of it were then closed and the ambulance drove off.

Walter, Vincent and Veronique returned to the apartment and Walter offered to leave them in peace but they both told him to stay for a while. He agreed, and finding glasses in their kitchen, poured three very large brandies. They sat in a row on the floor, backs to a sofa, facing the fire which Vincent had built and lit.

Veronique was calmer now and Vincent breathed a long smoky sigh of relief. He'd lit a cigarette for Veronique too, but she hadn't touched it.

"Walter," he said. "Thank you for what you did. My goodness me, you were quick. I guess that's army training for you."

"Yes, I suppose," said Walter. "Probably best we don't call the police. Is that okay?" said Walter. They both nodded.

"You got them good," said Vincent.

"Veronique, are you feeling better?" Walter asked. She looked at Vincent.

"Walter," said Vincent. "Many years ago, the same thing happened to us. It was a very different part of Paris, and we were very poor and very young. We were walking home from a night out and we were attacked by a number of youths. I tried to fight back- and yes, so did Veronique too- but we had no chance; none at all. They continued to kick us long after we were both on the ground, and both unconscious. I was in hospital for two days after that. I don't even remember getting there. Veronique was in hospital for a month. She had a fractured skull. And she'd lost our baby. She was pregnant, and following the attack, and the miscarriage and resulting complications, we could never have another child."

Walter nodded, deeply touched by the story. If ever there were two people in this world who would have made wonderful parents, it was Vincent and Veronique. It was heart-breaking.

"I wish you'd been my parents," was all he could say. He just blurted it out and immediately knew the remark sounded silly given age and his past with Veronique.

Walter was in awe of their ability to get on with life in the face of such tragedy, and without exacting revenge. He questioned his own view of the world. If it was him, he'd have dedicated years to finding every one of those muggers and exacting revenge. And yet, would he have been any happier if he had? He had to say, the answer was probably yes. There are some things you can't ignore. They say that it takes strength to forgive. Did that mean he was weak? No, he wasn't. That was the problem with sayings, most of them were rubbish.

"Did they ever find the people who did that to you?" he asked.

"No, never."

"Did you look for them yourselves?"

"No, Walter, we didn't. You know, if someone had given me a gun and lined them up against a wall, I'd have shot them, for sure. I really would. But hunting them ourselves, then killing them- if we could find them- and if we could kill them- what was the point? We would still have been sad, and just as bad as them. Instead, we left our jobs and went to the south coast for a year. I worked in a restaurant and Veronique took a break from her studies. She worked in the bar, in the same restaurant I worked in, and over time, we grew strong and happy again, then returned to Paris to get on with our lives."

Walter took this all in. They had chosen a future with just the two of them.
"Are you happy?" He regretted asking the question as soon as he'd blurted it out. It was clumsy. But he was curious.

"Yes, we are, Walter," said Veronique. "Does that surprise you? It does, doesn't it?"

"It's just such a sad story. And so unnecessary."

"It is, yes." said Vincent. "Sometimes life leaves you with stark choices, Walter. In our case, we could live under a cloud, or move on and live under the sun. We chose the sun." That was the second time Walter had heard such an analogy. Maybe they were right, and he was wrong. Maybe revenge isn't all it's made out to be.

"One day I will have children," he said. "And when I do, you will be their Godparents. Both of you. To every child I have."

They drank to that.

Chapter 27. Cooking Fish, Paris, Summer 1978.

Graduation from chef school had been a great thing for Walter. He was now a superb chef, and this gave him a great deal of satisfaction. He had decided to take up two offers from Vincent and Veronique, one from each of them.

He was offered a job as a line chef in charge of fish at a small restaurant which lay a little off the beaten track in the northern part of the city. This was not tourist country according to Vincent, so he'd have the demanding palettes of real people to deal with. Walter thought that tourists were real people too, but he understood what Vincent meant. The only thing in the world that Walter didn't like eating was fish, of course, but he decided that the job would be good for him and would give him time to think about his future. He'd also have the opportunity to see first-hand if he enjoyed the restaurant world; he might decide to open one himself. Things change, plans change.

Having finished chef school, and after experiencing the pillows in Veronique's bed, he'd decided to spend a little more money on rent and had found a nice one-bedroom flat in the southern part of the city. This meant that each day he'd cross the Seine on his Vespa, once per day at mid-morning and once late at night on his return home. He'd use a different bridge on his way to work each day, and on his return home too, just because he could. There were thirty-seven bridges to choose from and while many were out of his way, he still chose to take them sometimes. The new apartment had a good-sized, well-equipped kitchen, and on his two days off each week, he'd make croissants- chocolate, almond and lemon ones (which he later stopped making because they were not good) and sweeter ones (which he also stopped making later- they were his own inventions, and they didn't work). Lesson learned. He'd stick to the traditional.

In a momentous step for him, he took up Veronique's offer to talk, but he wanted to do it in her office, not in her bed. He wasn't sure what he'd get out of talking but anything positive would be good, especially if he could get rid of the recurring dream. He was entering these sessions blindly, but his trust of Veronique and Vincent was now absolute, and there was good reason for it.

Two days after the mugging incident, it was reported in the press that two men had been badly injured by muggers. One had been found unconscious where Walter had left him. His friend with the damaged leg had told the police that he had no idea who had done this to them as they'd both been attacked from behind when walking home. It was a lie of course, but what else could he say? They were a pair of idiots.

Walter, who read newspapers each day, but had missed the article and had been told by Vincent and Veronique as they sat around a table drinking wine, the following week.

"We will never tell the police. Those muggers could have killed us, Walter." said Veronique, "next time knock them both out."

"They'll probably be out mugging someone else in the upcoming weeks" said Vincent, "but I have to say, if ever anything is likely to put them off doing it again, what you did would be it, Walter. It'll hopefully make them think twice about doing it again."

Walter said nothing, but nodded in agreement. He had vowed never to kill again and the night of the mugging, had worried that he might have killed the man he punched. If he'd knocked his head on the pavement it could easily have happened.

He was, however, pleased that he was thinking this way, because his life was changing, and he needed to change too if he was going to find happiness. And so, it was time to talk to Veronique.

One morning, on one of his days off, Walter and Veronique laughed as they sat opposite each other in Veronique's consulting room and faced each other. The idea of embracing had occurred to them both, and they knew it, but great mind-reader as she was, Veronique told him:

"Not here, Walter." It was what Walter had thought too- before he saw her in person again. She really was beautiful. But this was business. He had some serious talking to do.

And now, getting to business, she explained to him that he was the only one who could resolve any issues he had. Her job was simply to show him the way.

"You and Vincent are the only people I've ever trusted who haven't let me down."

"How many people have you ever trusted, Walter?"

"Five."

"So not counting me and Vincent, it's three, is that correct?"

"Yes."

"And all three let you down?"

"Yes."

"And were your parents two of the three?"

"Yes."

"And the other?"

Walter waited a few weeks before talking of "the other." In the preceding weeks, he spoke of his childhood and leaving home. And of his need to keep a hammer close by, and how the habit had stuck with him- and served him well later in life. He spoke of the security and camaraderie of the army which had done him much good, and the feeling of accomplishment from chef school. When asked how he had so much money- for Veronique had been in his new apartment a number of times and knew it to be expensive- Walter said he'd inherited the money from a distant relative. He didn't like to lie to her, but the truth wouldn't help. Veronique, for her part, suspected that his story wasn't true but chose not to pursue the subject because it wouldn't help.

Walter eventually told Veronique of his recurring dream, and she was deeply touched by it, and like a jigsaw puzzle, she began to put together a picture of a badly burned Walter Mack. Literally, badly burned.

He showed her his armpits, and at that point she put her arms around him and cut short their session. She telephoned Vincent before leaving the office with Walter and told Vincent to meet them. Vincent knew his wife's voice well and did as she asked, dropping everything. He was needed. Whatever it was, it was important that he be there.

The three of them talked about good things and good people and good times. For hours, they ate well and drank too much. Walter slept in their spare room that night and thanked them in the morning for their kindness.

Eventually, Walter spoke to Veronique of Prudence, but to his surprise, on this particular subject Veronique was surprisingly matter of fact, and not particularly sympathetic, he felt. He was expecting a great deal of sympathy but instead he received none.

"Walter, I'm a quarter Moroccan. France is full of people of Moroccan ancestry, and I can tell you without any hesitation that there is no way on earth that Prudence's rich father would have been comfortable with his daughter being with you. He would have wanted a Moroccan boy or even perhaps an English boy who has been to the best of schools and is from one of the best families. Why he even let you meet her in the mornings for coffee is beyond me. That in itself is unusual for a rich Moroccan family. You said you did some work for the man: what kind of work was it?"

Walter's vague response about helping with security told Veronique not to probe any further on that subject. Walter definitely had some secrets, but everyone does; she knew that.

"Perhaps she didn't turn up on that last day because she didn't want to see you," she said. "Most likely her father was afraid you'd plan to abscond together in the future: who knows? Don't automatically think she abandoned you. Walter; you've jumped to the worst conclusion based on your childhood experiences. It's understandable of course, but have you tried contacting her, or going to Morocco to see her?"

"I can't go back to Morocco for security reasons- army security related issues," he lied. "I did try calling her over a few months last year but couldn't reach her. Then I gave up."

"Are you worried that she will reject you again if you manage to talk with her?" Walter said nothing, but Veronique could safely take that as a yes.

"Does she know you're in France?"

"No." he replied. This was surely true. Given what Veronique had just said, there was no way that Omar would have told her where he was.

"She must have meant the world to you, Walter. I don't know for sure what happened, of course. I'm a psychologist, so while I know lots about psychology, I'm not sure how much I really know about anything else. I've met doctors who know lots about medicine and nothing about people.

The reasons people do things or don't do them is still one of the world's great mysteries. The only advice I can give you is to either resolve the situation by contacting her or move on. Both will take courage of the sort you maybe haven't developed yet."

To Walter this was painful to hear, but he knew Veronique was just being honest with him.

"How can I put it?" she thought. "Your early years have left you so thin-skinned that it's see-through. But you can't attack everyone who annoys you. Or run from them. You need to grow a thicker skin, even try to enjoy the tough times. My father once said to me that life is like a flight on an aeroplane. There's the take-off, which is your birth, and the late years of your life, which is your landing. The bit in the middle is the journey that we call life. We all experience turbulence, but you've got to learn to accept it: drink a large whisky, settle into your seat and enjoy it. Admittedly, Walter, your take off was hideous: your plane nearly crashed and burned, but it didn't, Walter; you survived. So, get on with the rest of your journey."

An aeroplane ride, thought Walter on his way home. Given the people he'd met and the horror stories he'd heard he was beginning to wonder if he was a cry baby. He decided to think over Veronique's advice. He suspected that at some point he'd end up having to go to Morocco- somehow- to resolve things once and for all. But not now. He'd wait until his year in the restaurant was finished.

As his sessions with Veronique progressed, Walter talked more openly, and over time he had a feeling of progress. It was hard to explain, but perhaps it was just a feeling of being more settled within himself. More optimistic.
One day Veronique asked him what happiness looked like to him. He answered without hesitation:

"It's a small café of my own, somewhere the sun shines. It's peaceful and friendly. In the mornings it opens at 8am and closes at 11am. The only food available is fresh croissants made by me in my own oven- and to drink you can have either coffee or hot chocolate. Or tap water or grapefruit juice. In the afternoons it opens at 4pm and closes at 8pm. The only food available is bread, olives and Iberian ham. And for drinks, you can have wine, beer, champagne and perhaps something else I have in mind – a special cocktail."

"It sounds wonderful, Walter," said Veronique: "what will the café be called?"

"I don't know what it will be called, but it will soon have a name."

"It all makes so much sense, Walter. The sun. Your own café. Wonderful food. It sounds like a happy place. For you it will be a new dawn. You must do this."

Walter already knew that, but it meant everything to hear it from Veronique.

His future was set.

Chapter 28. Prudence. Paris. April 1979.

For over two years Prudence had worked in many bars and nightclubs around Malaga. Some of them she'd heard of from her father, some not. They were all run by the same kind of people. She'd used a false name and was paid in cash. No one knew who she was, and she didn't ask after Walter by name. She'd just worked, looked around, went to bars and cafés– places he'd likely be– travelled the region, and kept her eyes and ears open.

And so, after a while she'd settled into a routine: she'd leave a job, then spend a few weeks travelling along the coast, sometimes staying in a small town or village that looked appealing. Over the two years she spent on Spain's southern coast she'd looked out over the Atlantic Ocean and looked out over the Mediterranean towards Morocco, wondering if anyone there missed her.

She visited and worked in the Balearic Islands and while she liked the north end of Majorca, she didn't like the southern part of the island. She visited Menorca but didn't stay long.

Waking up one day she wondered why she'd spent so much time in Spain. She didn't even speak the language well and not having seen or heard anything that would indicate that Walter had been there, she decided to go to Paris where at least she could speak the language; and it may well be somewhere she could eventually settle if she decided to give up looking for him. That's if she ever decided to give up. Like Walter, she had nothing and no one, only memories of being with him and feeling like there was no one else in the world she wanted to be with. She decided to keep looking – what else did she have to do?

She bought a train ticket from Malaga to Paris.

Chapter 29. All gone. Paris, April 1979.

As he often did, one evening Walter decided to visit a Moroccan restaurant he loved, called Morocco. It wasn't an inspired name, but the food was fabulous. He'd once taken Vincent there to try the food, and he'd enjoyed it.

Walter was close to completing a year as a line-chef and had already handed in his notice. A year was enough. He was planning on moving south to the coast of the Mediterranean Sea where there were three hundred days of sunshine per year. He'd find a spot to build his café. He'd be twenty- nine years of age by then. He'd told Vincent and Veronique of his plans to leave, and they were both delighted for him, promising on their lives to come to the opening, whenever that would be. Walter knew that they'd keep their promise and be there.

He was welcomed at the door of Morocco restaurant by the manager who knew him well now, and ushered him into the bustling restaurant, showing him to an empty table for two. Without saying a word, the manager left, then swiftly returned with an ice cold beer. Walter thanked him, picked up the glass and took a long draft.

"Walter!" a voice boomed out from behind him. He turned to see a face he knew well.

"Hello Walter." It was the bodyguard who used to accompany Prudence whenever she met Walter in Marrakech, the man who worked for Omar. Walter realised that he'd never learned the man's name. Now, this was a coincidence.

"Hey, don't you remember me? Tarik."

"I do indeed remember you, Tarik." said Walter looking around the restaurant to see who else from Marrakech might be there.

"I'm here with my family for dinner." He pointed to a table in the corner of the restaurant. A nice looking woman and two young children, a boy and a girl, waved over at him. Walter waved back.

"What are you doing in Paris, Tarik?"

"I live here now. I no longer work for Omar; that all came to an end."

"Sorry to hear that. What happened?"

"I can't believe that you don't know." Walter eyed Tarik closely, keenly interested.

"After Prudence disappeared, Omar had no need for a bodyguard for her, so I was out of a job. I've got extended family here, so decided to move here. My wife has family here too."

The two men were standing in the middle of the restaurant so Walter asked Tarik if he could have a quick moment to chat to him. Tarik agreed and sat down at Walter's table after going to his own table and telling his wife he'd be back in a minute.

"I knew that Prudence had disappeared, Tarik. She'd been kidnapped, but she was returned, yes?" Walter was alarmed and confused.

"I don't think you know what's happened, my friend." said Tarik.

"Tell me. It sounds like I know very little."

"Well, I'm not sure you will really want to know this, Walter- but I'll tell you all the same."

He sat back and looked Walter in the eye as Walter's stomach tightened.

"On your last day in Marrakech, Omar forcibly kept Prudence in the house. He was worried she would run off with you, or plan to meet you in the future. The truth is, he respected you, but he didn't want you as his son-in-law." Tarik shrugged his shoulders.

"The day after you'd gone, an envelope arrived for her, the one which had the photograph of you both. I saw it. Prudence was waving it in her father's face, screaming at him. She went crazy, but by the time he eventually relented and let her out of the house, you had gone. He wouldn't tell her how to reach you. She started acting foolishly, you know, going out late at night, trying to get away from me- my job was to look after her, make sure she was safe. But it got harder and harder. She spent every moment trying to escape from me. I started to feel bad. She was so upset. Time rolled on, but nothing improved.

Eventually she and Omar did not speak to each other any longer. The atmosphere in that house was horrible. Months dragged by. Then one day, when we were out, she was kidnapped- this you do know. I was drinking coffee on a restaurant terrace close to where she was sitting when she went to the restroom- but she never came back. She'd been taken." He paused. "Luckily, whatever it is that you did, Walter, it secured her release. I was the one who collected her when she was freed, and I was there when she was reunited with Omar. He was over the moon to see her, but she didn't really seem to care. It was only when Omar said he needed to call you that she came back to life. He telephoned you, but it seems that you only spoke with Prudence for a second or two; I don't know what happened, but she became sad again. Did you hang up on her, Walter?"

"Keep going please, Tarik." Walter was feeling sick.

"Well, she fought with her father again and he refused to give her any information about how to contact you or where you were. All he said was that you were now living in North America under an assumed name. Or maybe he mentioned Quebec, but either way, he said that she would never see you again. I witnessed all of it, and it was very sad to see. I'd heard you were actually in Spain but at the time it was more than my job was worth to tell Prudence, so I had said nothing."

Tarik paused and took a deep breath.

"The next part is even worse. That evening, on witnessing such a sad scene, I decided to tell Prudence that I'd heard you were in Spain, not Quebec. It felt like the right thing to do. However, I wasn't going to have an opportunity to talk to her until the following morning. The next day when I arrived at the house there was chaos. Prudence had left. By the time we tracked her to the airport, she was already on a flight to Spain. But from there, we discovered she'd flown to Canada. We spent two months looking for her. Believe me, our connections are good- we have friends everywhere- but we couldn't find her. We suspect that somehow, she got hold of a false passport. It's perfectly possible because there are many ways to do that in Marrakech. Maybe she got one in Canada. We don't know. We looked high and low but came up with nothing. Walter, my friend; she's gone."

"I will kill Omar for this," he replied. Walter wasn't exaggerating.

"No need. He died from a heart attack. I heard that through friends of mine. Omar fired me shortly after he gave up on finding Prudence. That's when I decided to come here. His business interests were taken over by friends and rivals alike, and I didn't want to work for them. Everything is gone. It was as if Omar and Prudence had never existed. Even Omar's house has been taken over. It's very sad. Prudence was a wonderful girl. She deserved more, but the world can be the cruellest of places."

The two men looked at each other, reflecting on this sad state of affairs. It was a shocking one for Walter, and he was deeply saddened.

He thanked Tarik and wished him and his family good luck for the future. He accepted the offer to stay in touch but knew it wouldn't happen because he was soon to be leaving Paris.

"I can see the sadness in your eyes, Walter. I'm sorry that it was left to me to tell you such news. I wish we hadn't met tonight. I think that might have been better."

Walter left the restaurant without eating, never to return.

Chapter 30. Prudence. Paris. The same night, same place, same time.

Prudence had arrived in the city of light a week previously. Years before she'd visited Paris but was awash with money then– how times had changed. On this evening in April 1979, as she was out walking, trying to get a feel for the city from an impoverished person's perspective, she passed a restaurant called Morocco and tried to see inside but it was busy and the way the restaurant was shaped, she could only see the reception area which led to the main dining room. She looked inside longingly, wishing she had enough money to dine inside and feast on some of her beloved Moroccan food. But she didn't, so she walked on and bought cigarettes instead, unaware that inside the restaurant, Walter and Tariq were talking about her.

The next day Walter lay in bed feeling sorry for himself, and for Prudence too. What a price both he and she were paying for his anger. If only he hadn't hung up on her.

The next day, Prudence walked the streets looking for work, eventually finding a job in a place called Bar Pic where an extraordinarily unpleasant woman called Helen worked. It was the only bar in Paris which Walter would never go to.

Chapter 31. Moving On. Paris, June 1979.

Over the weeks that passed, Walter racked his brains wondering how he might find Prudence. She was possibly alone and in need of his help. Even if she didn't need him, he now knew that she wanted him. He was disgusted with himself for the lack of self-confidence he'd shown.

The problem he faced in trying to find her was that he couldn't use his contacts in the military- the first thing he'd thought of- because there were rules about not using military lines of communications for private purposes and those lines wouldn't be crossed.

All sorts of ideas occurred to him: he could hire a private detective or contact various immigration services. However, if she was using a false passport or had gone into hiding, wherever she was, the task of finding her was almost impossible. You needed Interpol for a job like this. And, if he was being honest with himself, he knew that if Omar's network couldn't find her, how could he, Walter Mack? He could of course put an advert in the newspapers. Or could he? Which ones – the Canadian ones? They probably wouldn't run the ad even if he paid for it unless it was in the classifieds, but she likely wouldn't see it. No matter which idea he came up with, it seemed to be flawed. He could think of nothing that might work. And now with Omar dead and his network broken up, Prudence wouldn't be able to use it to find him, even if she wanted to. Walter despaired and tried to move on with life, once again.

He spent his final days in Paris picking himself up, and cleaning the apartment, returning the keys, cancelling gas and electricity, and planning his route south. He'd bought a good map detailing the back roads throughout the country and worked out where his first week on the road might take him. His little Vespa wouldn't be allowed on main roads which suited him well. There was no hurry. He'd researched the southern coastline and identified twelve old villages over an area of about fifty square miles that he decided he'd stay at, in an effort to find the perfect spot to open his café. At the very least, it would be a good starting place.

His final dinner with Veronique and Vincent was good, enabling him to leave the city in the right frame of mind. He had decided not to tell them about Prudence because it was all too complicated without telling the whole truth, and in this case, it was something he couldn't do. He was leaving a lover, his best friends, and his mentors. It was sad, but he was so very lucky to have met them. He promised them an invitation to the opening of his café, and they promised him, as they'd done many times before, that they'd be there. He also promised them that until the day he died, he would see them at least once per year. Hopefully more often. His final promise to them was an invitation to join him for Christmas day, perhaps a year or so from now, once he'd found himself somewhere nice to live. That might take a bit of time, but it would happen. He wouldn't abandon them.

For his journey south, Walter had everything he needed: his Vespa, a change of clothes, cigarettes, map, money, and sunglasses. What more would he need?

He climbed onto his scooter at just past 6am on a beautiful morning and took a deep breath. Everything he owned in the world was with him, and he needed nothing more for now. He'd lost the love of his life, for that's surely what Prudence was- and it would burn him forever- but in Vincent and Veronique he'd gained friends better than any he could have ever hoped for, and through that, he'd gained a little faith in people, and life.

He had his training from the army, and all that had done for his confidence and sense of belonging. He had his newfound wealth, and he was a very well-trained young chef. He had everything he needed to begin a new life. Not bad for a young lad from Edinburgh. Time to live.

He started the scooter and sped through the streets of Paris, the rising sun warming the left side of his face, even at this early hour. He was the dawn itself. Life was starting anew.

Chapter 32. South, June 1979.

Walter's Vespa could manage a top speed of sixty kilometres per hour, so he knew the journey south would take time- something that he wanted it to do. His nature was often to push things to the maximum, so if he was in a fast car for example, or on a powerful motor bike he'd have raced down the motorways, likely in one day. The country roads he was using and the little Vespa allowed him to enjoy the views which became more beautiful the further south he went.

Two hours out of Paris, and pretty much using the sun and some bad road signage to guide him– not his map- Walter stopped for petrol at a tiny station that was in the middle of nowhere. It was an Elf station, and Walter looked at the sign as he refuelled, thinking about the fabulous Mixed Elves that Prudence had made for him in Morocco. The name hadn't made any sense at all, but that was one of the reasons he liked it. He'd loved the taste, and so while filling the petrol tank he decided that he'd definitely add Mixed Elves to the limited drinks menu that would be available when he opened his café, wherever and whenever that might be. He'd been thinking of adding them to the menu for a while, and he saw the Elf station as a sign confirming that he should do it. It would also be a small, but deeply personal tribute to Prudence. They'd always remind him of her.

Having accepted that she was gone, he wanted to think happily of her, not with regret. He was embarrassed by the depth of his self-pity over his loss. He must have been so very boring for Veronique to listen to.

He saw postcards for sale in the tiny shop where he paid for his petrol, so he bought one, and a stamp, and wrote to Veronique and Vincent: "Following the sun! All good so far. More news soon. Walter."

With nowhere booked to sleep that night, he drove on past various hospitality options, with none appealing to him until just past seven pm when he came to a village with a small bed and breakfast. He'd done close to a hundred and fifty kilometres, which meant that he'd been travelling very slowly indeed, stopping often, sometimes just to look at the scenery, and not really making much of a dent in the journey: perfect.

The bed and breakfast looked clean and well-kept and offered an evening meal which suited him well. The proprietors of the old two-story detached building at the side of the road were an old couple who looked like twins.

Walter was hungry and pleasantly tired. At eight pm, having moved his few belongings from the scooter to his room, Walter sat down at the kitchen table to enjoy dinner with the old couple. The man, like the woman, looked at Walter very suspiciously over the top of his spectacles, leading Walter to wonder if he looked to others like a shady character. He didn't think so.

A plate was put down in front of him and to his delight, it contained a Charolais steak; his favourite cut which he knew was very expensive. It was cooked to perfection and he couldn't help but wonder if the old lady had attended the Cordon Bleu school decades before he had. He complimented the couple on the food and enjoyed some fabulously rustic wine along with the steak. He told them he was travelling south very slowly, chasing the sun. They smiled at this, telling him, as many before them had, that the south had three hundred days of sunshine per year.

His bed was like a hammock though, and his feet were higher off the ground than his head, while his backside was almost on the floor. But rotten mattress or not, he didn't sleep too badly, the fresh air having done more than any sleeping pill could have done.

He woke at 6am and lay still in his rotten bed, enjoying the sounds of the old couple moving about downstairs making breakfast. When the smell of coffee wafted upstairs, he could stay in bed no longer, so he got up, washed, shaved, and headed down for some more food, planning to brush his teeth after he'd eaten.

He asked the old lady if she made the fabulous croissants herself, but she shook her head and said they were too troublesome. She bought them from a shop in the village owned by her twin sister.

Unbelievable; she had a twin, but it wasn't the man. He must be her husband. Perhaps the two old proprietors were just two kindred souls who had grown similar in looks over the years. Walter ate more than he should have but forgave himself because he was on holiday, and on paying and then thanking the old couple after brushing his teeth, he set off again.
The plan was to go further today, and perhaps veer off track slightly, spending a night or two in a village or small town. The sun was out again, accompanied by a light breeze.

He'd left at 9am driving just as slowly as he had done the day before, having abandoned the plan to travel faster this day. He was enjoying the beautiful solitude of the roads too much to think of speeding up much at all. There was no point.

Just after 2pm as he rounded yet another bend and came onto a long straight road shaded by plane trees, a figure on the side of the road up ahead of him appeared, dressed in a red dress with her arm out and thumb stuck up in the universally recognised hitchhiker's sign. Walter pulled up beside her. She was pretty. Long, dark curly hair and brown eyes, and a lovely smile. He asked if she was alright. She was, she said, but her car had broken down nearby and she needed a lift to the next village a few kilometres ahead. Walter said he'd happily give her a lift but his scooter had very little power so she shouldn't expect a speedy journey. She said it was fine and climbed onto the scooter behind him. They took off and she held on to him as he accelerated. A couple of hundred meters into the journey he saw a razor out of the corner of his eye and felt it rest against his throat.

"You'll see my boyfriend at the side of the road shortly. Stop there. If you do as you're told, and hand over your money, you won't get hurt."

Walter nodded in understanding. Looking ahead he could now see the boyfriend.

As they approached him, the girl shouted at Walter to slow down but he kept going, putting two fingers up at the boyfriend as he sped past.

The razor dug further into his throat but didn't break the skin. Walter continued.

"Let me off!" the girl shouted.

She continued to shout at him for a full minute before giving up, at which point she burst out laughing, and Walter laughed too. He was in a wicked mood and wasn't finished.

He sped on, going far too quickly for her to jump off. She withdrew the razor and started laughing again as Walter and his scooter zipped on.

No traffic lights, cars, tractors or roundabouts- nothing at all stopped Walter, and the girl was unable to get off. After about five kilometres he tired of the game and pulled up abruptly. The girl jumped off the scooter and looked around. She was in the middle of nowhere, perhaps an hour's walk from where she'd boarded the scooter.

Walter looked at her, knowing she could easily hitch a lift all the way back. He wondered if her boyfriend would wait for her.

She looked back at Walter and made another universally- recognised sign with her hand, this time the one that meant "crazy", and then turned and started walking- without her razor. It was tucked into Walter's jacket pocket.

She shouted "crazy guy" after him as he took off: the irony of being dumped in the middle of nowhere by someone on a motor bike hadn't escaped Walter.

After clearing his head, Walter looked at his watch and then the petrol gauge and saw that it was time to refuel and get some lunch. He hadn't really needed his watch because his stomach was rumbling which was all the prodding he needed. He sped up; his Vespa much lighter than it had been for the past few kilometres.

Having refuelled then travelled further south, he eventually took a turn off to a village signposted ten kilometres west of Lafat in the general direction he was going. He liked the sound of the name of the village, which meant Sleepy River so he felt he should probably just stop for the day. A walk or a run after a nap but before dinner, would do him some good. Just like the village he'd stayed at the night before it wasn't clear why the village existed as there were no signs of industry, but it was most likely an agricultural farming community given the surrounding fields- and perhaps some tourism too. It was certainly quaint, and as sleepy as the name suggested, with a gently flowing river that ran through its middle.

He parked and locked his scooter, then walked through the village, finding a café to eat at. He ate lightly, only having some ham and cheese and a small bottle of beer to quench his thirst. He asked the waitress if she knew of somewhere he might spend the night, and she pointed him in the direction of a small hotel which she said had three or four bedrooms. Apparently, it was run by an English couple, something the woman thought he'd like. He appreciated her kind thoughts and on finishing his food, he set off to find the hotel.

It faced the sleepy river and looked to be perfect for Walter's needs. It was much more expensive than the bed and breakfast he'd stayed at the night before, but he felt he deserved a treat having been threatened earlier in the day.

The owner of the hotel, Mrs Fox was indeed English, as was her husband, but he had died earlier in the year. It was odd that the woman in the café didn't know this because the village was so small, but on talking to Mrs Fox he found out that Mr Fox had died in England of a terminal illness. They'd spent his last months in England during the winter and she'd seen no need to broadcast the news when she returned. Those at the church knew, and that was plenty. Everyone else would find out over time.

Walter hadn't meant to pry, but he'd mentioned on checking in that he'd been told that the proprietors were an English couple. She waved off his apologies:

"He was lovely, but there's more than one person in the world for all of us, Mr Mack, so maybe I'll meet someone else someday."

Walter felt that was a little cold given that the man hadn't been in the ground for very long, but yes, he'd heard people say that before; there's more than one person out there for all of us: the trouble is finding them.

Mrs Fox turned out to be a friendly and kind person in her forties, who reminded Walter of the actor, Joan Collins. She had a complexion on her that Walter had seen before in Brits living where the sun shines- a healthy tone to her skin, more permanent than a tan. It was a slowly cooked hue, similar to the one Walter sported now, unlike the pasty white he'd worn before arriving in Morocco.

Mrs Fox showed Walter to his room, and he was delighted to see that it was large and clean. She asked if he'd be joining the other guests for dinner. Walter declined, saying that he was travelling by scooter and really wasn't appropriately dressed to be in the hotel's dining room.

"Not a problem- we eat outside in the garden at the back. It's lovely. And very casual. Shall I reserve a table for one for you Walter, or shall I make it a table for two?"

"I'll be on my own, Mrs Fox– and since you make the garden dining sound so appealing, I'll have a table please- but just for one thank you."

"This may sound rude, Mr Mack, and please don't think I'm implying anything, but would you be open to me joining you? It's a while since I've sat down and enjoyed some new company. Our guests fly in and fly out, it's pretty much work twenty-four hours a day. I'd like an evening off with a handsome and polite young man."

"That would be fabulous, Mrs Fox. Yes, please join- but only if you allow me to pay for dinner. I wouldn't want you to feel obliged to pay. You are a kind person. This, I can tell."

"That's a deal." she said. "Thank you. See you at 8pm."

She closed the door behind her, and Walter lay on his nice firm bed for a nap but found himself less tired than he thought; he went out and ran for an hour to get his lungs pumping and build up an appetite. He had a bath when he got back to the hotel, and then lay down on the bed again, this time to look at the map and add a little more planning to his journey. He could go on for days, drifting from village to village if he wanted to, but perhaps after all, it'd be best if he just gets on with things and try to find the place to build his café. Depending on where he was and the property or piece of land he bought, he wanted his café to be up and running within 12 months.

He had lots to do.

He'd need to open a local bank account, transfer funds, find a lawyer and an accountant, get a business license, find a property or a plot of land, renovate it or build on it, buy and install the right equipment he'd need, find the right suppliers of quality ingredients he wanted, buy furniture. Yes, lots to do, but all of it good.

He was certain of the menu now, and opening hours. His café was going to be pretty unique in terms of both. They were primarily for his enjoyment, but if others benefitted, great. The business plan was simple: break even. No profit needed. No loss wanted. Just break even.

The setting was to be somewhere that people had easy access to, but he would prefer locals more than tourists as customers. He didn't want the place overrun by demanding and pushy visitors. It should be within walking distance from his home, so he'd need to buy a house nearby. Did he want a house near to his café or a café near to his house? Not sure yet. Both, he supposed.

The café would have indoor and outdoor seating, perhaps enough for ten people inside and ten people outside, or a few more. But not a lot more.

He wondered what music he'd play, if any. Music could be intensely polarising. Maybe no music then- or if there was some, it should be present but barely audible; no pop. He knew nothing of classical music except that he loved the mellow tones that a cello produced. He wondered if he could find someone to come in and play. The most important thing was that people should always leave happy.

The southern coast of the country, and twenty kilometres inland along the coast, was littered with villages. His search was going to be about trade-offs between locals, tourists, scenery, available land and property, including his home, but most importantly, the feel of the place. Sleepy River, where he was now, felt nice but it wouldn't be right for Walter, even if it was down south. It was nice-looking but lacked character.

8pm floated close and he ambled downstairs and out onto the terrace at the back of the hotel where a waitress led him to his table. Mrs Fox wasn't there yet, so Walter said he'd wait for his guest to arrive before ordering a drink.

"Hello," said Mrs Fox as she approached the table seconds after the waitress had left. Walter stood and shook her hand.

"That's very formal," she said, "we tend to kiss each other on the cheek here."

"Ah, but I don't know you well," said Walter, thinking that there were very few people he'd ever kissed at all.

The waitress had reappeared and so he ordered a bottle of beer, and she, a gin and tonic.

"Very British," she said of her choice.

He smiled and they touched glasses. Walter looked at the menu and complimented Mrs Fox on it. He noticed that there was only one menu on the table which lay in front of him, and so he passed it to her. "Please you look first; though I'm assuming you already know what's on it?"

"Yes, I'm badly dyslexic anyway so I'd probably never make head or tail of it if I tried to read it. Reading in a foreign language- oh my lord. Some days I just want to give up. So generally, I remember things well. It's when it comes to reading and writing that things become a challenge."

Walter put down the menu and said he'd go for her recommendation in that case. The talk over dinner was easy, and he enjoyed Mrs Fox's company. He asked her if she'd stay and run the hotel, now that Mr. Fox had passed away.

"Oh yes. Definitely. This is my home now. I may not be old, but I feel that there's no need to make any changes to my life. I miss my husband, but he died happy, and so will I."

"You sound very sure of that," said Walter. He was interested in the idea of happiness, given that it was pretty much alien to him. He'd seen it in Veronique and Vincent, and the way he'd felt when he was with Prudence, but it just seemed to be so short-lived – almost conditional- as if it came at a special price, a limited offer only.

"I married my husband against the wishes of everyone I knew, including my entire family," she said, "no-one liked him. He was poor and uneducated. And rough round the edges."

"Well," said Walter, sitting up and feeling offended on behalf of Mr. Fox, and indeed himself, "that seems very unfair: harshly judgmental."

"It was. So, I married him all the same and we were really happy. He worked hard, and we worked well together. Over time everyone I knew, including my family, grew to like him but of course my husband was always wary of them. Why on earth would he not be?"

"Understandable."

"I think people were just trying to be protective of me, but they never seemed to listen to what I was saying. It was all about what they wanted for me, not what I wanted for myself. But in the end, I married the love of my life, and because of that, I'll die happy, whether I meet someone else or not."

"That is a great outlook on life," said Walter, sounding patronising but not meaning to be so.

"And what of you, Walter- what's your life story?"

As usual, it took Walter about thirty seconds to tell his entire life story. He really needed to work on it because his evasive answers sounded borderline offensive; a clear indication he didn't want to tell the person he was talking to anything at all.

Mrs Fox was great company, and very smart. She knew that the less she asked Walter, the more he'd tell her, and so he did. She also felt that as confident and buttoned down as he seemed to be, there was an underlying sadness in his eyes. Life hadn't been easy.

Dessert arrived and it was eaten completely because it was superb. A basic staple of any dessert menu, creme brûlée, was easy to make badly and very difficult to make well. Just like the croissant. Mrs Fox's team knew how to cook.

"Have you ever been in love, Walter?"

"Yes, I have." It was the first time he'd heard himself say "yes" to that question.

"What made you fall in love with her?"

"She was nice to me."

"Oh Walter! That's the saddest thing I ever heard. Just, nice?"

"Nice was something new to me at the time, but I know what you mean. I can't really describe it. I just wanted to be with her all the time."

"It sounds like she's gone now?" said Mrs Fox. Walter nodded.

"Plenty of fish in the ocean," she said. Another unhelpful saying thought Walter, but she was trying to be kind.

During what he called the brandy course, he told Mrs Fox of his plans to open a café in the sun, an idea she loved. She offered to help with the business side of it, especially in the start-up phase.

Walter only had to call when he was ready and she'd either talk him through things on the phone, or she'd happily drive down for a week or so to help.

Walter thanked her and promised that he'd call her for help, and that she'd be invited to the opening. She promised to help, and to be there, just like Veronique and Vincent.

It was a good evening all round, and Walter felt good about meeting Mrs. Fox. He was collecting friends like nobody's business now. He had three.

The following morning after a good breakfast of figs and coffee, he hugged Mrs Fox- he was getting used to hugging now too- and promised her that he'd be in touch as soon as he had settled and started the process of looking for a site for the café, and a home. She told him that he had better do that or she'd be coming down south to ask him why he hadn't done it. Full of energy, he kick-started the scooter, and sped off.

Chapter 33. Making haste. France. 1st July 1979.

It would probably take somewhere between eighteen and twenty-four hours to get down to Nice, Walter calculated.

He'd made up his mind to complete the rest of his journey as quickly as possible, even if that meant driving all through the night. His long conversation with Mrs Fox had intensified his desire to get the café up and running. The plan of slowly meandering was now dropped, and the attempted mugging by the girl and her useless boyfriend had soured things a little.

The kilometres, the time, and the countryside all sped by, and he only stopped to refuel, and drink lots of water. He needed an hour out of the midday sun after leaving Sleepy River though, because while the breeze rushing over him as he motored kept him cool superficially, he'd eventually burn if he didn't find some shade.

He found a nice spot in a field off the road, sitting with his back against an old plane tree. He studied the map and was delighted with the good progress he was making on his fabulous Vespa, limited in speed as it was. He'd continue as fast as he could after his break in the shade, and after the sandwiches he'd bought. The sandwiches tasted good and when he'd finished them, he decided to close his eyes.

Before he knew it, he was half awake, half asleep, in that no man's land of being, and he was thinking of his childhood. It wasn't the recurring dream, but his time at school. He saw himself back in Latin classes where he had two teachers that taught him the subject on alternate days. It was the only subject that held any interest for him at all, and that was not because he enjoyed grammar or declensions. He loved the stories that came with the course. They transported him away from the bitter loneliness he lived in, to another world, somewhere he wanted to be, despite how dangerous those times were.

Virgil's Aeneid- a poem that he'd dreaded reading before he started it because it was so long- turned out to be his favourite. At school they weren't expected to read the whole thing, just selected pieces, but what they did read, he found intriguing. And yet now, years later, he couldn't remember any of it, only that he'd loved it and it had become an escape for him, somewhere to dream of. It seemed such an odd thing that now, as an adult, he could remember loving the stories but couldn't remember the detail of them, other than they featured great sea journeys, brave warriors, fights against the most fearsome of wild beasts, and battles won, and battles lost. It was odd what the memory retained and what it didn't.

At school, he hated seeing the bullying of weaker people, and remembered one poor lad who was always being challenged to fights for no other reason than he was a poor fighter. Knowing beforehand that he'd lose, this lad would turn up to the fight in his waterproof mac to stop blood running from his nose onto his uniform.

There was one especially nasty teen, perhaps thirteen or fourteen years old, who was always after the weaker ones, and loved to hurt the boy in the mac. And yet, one day, the nasty little bully didn't turn up for school, and indeed never returned at all because he'd been murdered in a gang fight. Walter was happy. He knew that he wasn't supposed to be happy when someone died, but what he was supposed to feel and what he actually felt were very different. He couldn't help it. The "supposed to" part didn't change Walter's mind, and it was at this point in his life that he started to believe a little more in himself and what his gut told him, versus what people told him he was supposed to think. Walter didn't believe he'd ever conform.

When it came time to leave school for good, it was an internal clock that told him, not a school timetable. A school bell had gone off, but not outside for everyone to hear, only in his head. One day he walked out of the school and never looked back. And here he was now, under the shade of a beautiful plane tree– snoozing or daydreaming, though it didn't matter which it was. Soon, he'd build a café. And then a house, a place that for the first time in his life would feel like home, not just be called home.

Chapter 34. Mougins, July 1979.

He wondered how long it might take his scooter to carry him up the long hill that led to the old village. It was incredibly steep, even steeper than the roads that led to other villages close to the coast that he'd visited in the previous weeks. He felt thankful that he wasn't walking. This road was so steep that his scooter was close to stalling. He'd been wise enough to wait until late afternoon to explore this village: late afternoon visits now being a routine that he'd decided upon after a sweltering mid-day visit to the village of Tourrettes-sur-Loup a few days earlier.

Mougins would be the eleventh village he'd visited on his list of twelve. Like many of the villages in this part of the world, it had a fabulously interesting history- and a small population of around nine thousand people, but many visitors on a daily basis, especially in the warm months. They were mostly tourists and wealthier people from other parts of Europe who owned property nearby. Festivals were held in the village each year and it had a heritage of culinary excellence as well as a long line of well-known celebrity residents from days gone by, including Picasso. On eventually reaching the village, Walter loved the look of it but wondered if it might just be too busy for him and possibly more expensive than he might want. The views were stunning, the architecture wonderful, and there was an ambience that was just right. Interesting.

After a walk round around the centre and the back streets, Walter sat on the edge of a fountain, waiting for the sun to drop a little bit further before finding somewhere to have a cold beer and watch the sunset. A dog approached him.

"Hello," said Walter.

The dog came right up to him, without any hesitation, and sat down to have his head scratched. Walter looked around to see who the owner was, but no-one seemed to own him- it was indeed a boy, because he was now cocking his leg against the fountain wall. He's a lovely boy, thought

Walter: like a sheep dog, with a black and white coat and a personality that was full of curiosity and life.

A good fifteen minutes went by as Walter looked around from time to time for an owner, and as he did, his new friend sat beside him. It was as if they'd known each other for years. They were very relaxed in each other's company. Still, no one came by to claim the dog though, and Walter wondered what to do. He heard the loud rattling of shutters being pulled down and looked around to see the tourist office closing, so he walked over to the young lady who was closing up shop. He asked her who owned the dog, explaining that it had just come to sit with him. In fact, was the dog hers? The woman was about the same age as himself, Walter thought, and pretty, and polite. She told Walter that the dog had just appeared in the village a week or so back. She brushed back the blond hair that had fallen in front of her face, telling him that the dog seemed to be a stray that picked up scraps of food wherever he could. She put out water for him sometimes to stop him jumping into the fountain to drink. He was a friendly dog ,she said, but a waif.

"Just like me," thought Walter.

"Can I take him?" He asked her.

"Well, I suppose you can." she said. "He doesn't seem to belong to anyone. It would be nice if you could give him a home. What will you call him?"

Walter thought about that. "Vincent," he said.

She said she liked the name and watched Walter and Vincent head down the slope to the car park, to Walter's scooter.

With absolutely no trouble at all, Walter managed to get Vincent sitting calmly on the back of the scooter and the pair of them trundled off slowly back towards the small hotel that Walter was staying at in a neighbouring village.

His room opened onto a small courtyard, so he hoped that having Vincent wouldn't be a problem for the owners, and it turned out that it wasn't. The dog was fabulous, friendly and house trained, and so in a fit of good consciousness the next day, Walter decided to post a flyer at the tourist office in Mougins, saying that he had the dog, and the owner could collect him. A dog this well-trained and friendly had been looked after in the past and was no doubt missed badly by someone; someone who would surely be out looking for him.

Both Walter and Vincent went to the tourist office to see the same woman Walter had spoken with the day before. Her name was Jo. Having found some writing paper in his hotel room Walter had written a short but clear note, so that if the owner happened to read it, he or she would know exactly what to do. Jo agreed to post the notice outside the office. Thanking her, Walter headed off with Vincent.

A full week went by. Each day, Walter would walk Vincent in the morning, then leave him in the courtyard outside his room with shade and water. Walter would only ever be away for a few hours at time, at most, and he would come home to a hero's welcome from Vincent. On the last day of the week, with no one claiming Vincent, Walter phoned the tourist office and spoke with Jo who suggested that if no one had claimed the dog by now, then it was unlikely to happen. Walter should take the dog knowing he was doing the right thing. Walter was delighted. Yet another friend!

For a month, Walter travelled around the region looking beyond his first twelve choices for the perfect village in which to build his café. The twelve villages on his list were good, but the only one that came anywhere near to what he was looking for was Mougins. However, he had decided that the old village on top of the hill would be too busy, and too expensive, but that perhaps he could buy somewhere at the foot of the hills if he could find the right spot. It was much less busy lower down because it wasn't where tourists stopped. The lower levels would have mostly local footfall, or foreign residents who knew the area. It was still fabulously scenic, but much less of a climb than the old village. The only problem was, there didn't seem to be any good views. Logically, though, the lower he went, the less chance there would be of finding a spot with a good view. There had to be somewhere though: surely, if he just kept looking, he'd find what he wanted?

On the Tuesday morning, he visited a third estate agent and explained what he wanted to do. He tried two others, but neither had come up with any interesting properties, so he'd dropped them. This latest one was very helpful as all estate agents on the cusp of making money are expected to be, but it appeared to Walter that this one knew a lot more people who lived in the area personally, not just foreign homeowners wanting to rent or sell. This meant that given enough time, and some serious networking in the community they could likely find a good commercial property, a residential property or possibly parcels of land that may not currently be listed for sale. In simple terms, they could possibly find both the commercial and residential properties that Walter was looking for. That was good news.

He could tell that the estate agent, Mr Martin, was surprised that someone of his scant years had the money to make such expensive purchases but was too polite and too professional to ask directly if he had the money.

He did, however, try roundabout methods such as asking him if it was a business venture his parents were also involved in, and what the family business was, where his family resided and so on until he eventually decided to drop it. Walter revealed nothing but he was wise enough to recognise the direction of their questions, so rather than leave him in doubt which might lead to less effort on his part, he simply assured him that he understood the line of their questioning and that he had the means to pay for any purchases outright. No lending required. If his word wasn't good enough for them, he'd leave. Otherwise, he asked that he get on with things. The agent decided to get on with things.

Walter went with Mr Martin to first look at a number of residential properties as part of Mr Martin's wise decision to fully understand the kind of property Walter was looking for. It's easy to describe what you want, thought Walter; however, it's not so much about words but feeling when it comes to finding the right kind of place. So, Mr Martin was taking exactly the right approach. He'd get a feel for what Walter wanted.

The first day's scouting and understanding trip was positive, though not conclusive by any means. If Walter needed to look at a hundred places he would. An interesting suggestion Mr Martin had was to look carefully on the other side of the hill where Walter hadn't yet spent much time because it was on the opposite side of Mougins to the direction he approached the village from each day. While it was much lower than the village, some of the houses had fabulous views, something which wouldn't be obvious to the passersby because many of the properties were tucked away, back from the road and hidden behind trees. This was great news.

In terms of his future home, Walter felt that three bedrooms would do. In the remote case he might have more than one visitor at a time; three bedrooms would be ample. But perhaps it might just be wise to go for more? Why limit himself?

He'd need a huge ground floor providing enough space to build a large kitchen with space to sit and lounge around in. He wanted a garden at the back where he could plant olive trees and perhaps build a pool to exercise in. He'd need a private entrance where he could put in electric gates to ensure his home was secure. A view was a must- sea or hills- either would be good- and the house' exterior would need to have beautiful stonework.

This hopefully wasn't too much to ask, and it didn't seem complicated. And yet, while he saw one or two places that should have matched most of his needs, none of them felt right. As the days passed, Mr Martin gained a good understanding of Walter's feelings. In his opinion, he told Walter, it may well be that an unsolicited approach to one or two existing property owners might be the way forward. He had one specific residence in mind which was owned by an elderly couple from Paris whose adult children didn't seem to have much interest in the place, partly because there were several of them, and they all knew that squabbles would arise over its usage. The property and land would also be very expensive to maintain which would be off-putting for them. Walter was open to the idea of approaching them, and he asked Mr Martin to look into it. In the meantime, he should also start looking at commercial properties where he could build his café.

Very much like the residential property, there were many parcels of land and buildings available but few that came close to fitting the bill. Walter needed enough space inside for a number of people, space at the front, and back, as well as parking for two or three cars, but not too many more. And he needed enough land to make the garden and seating areas outside of his café truly beautiful. He had in his mind a garden at the front and one at the back too, both of which would be rich in colour and scented from all the flowers he planned to grow and care for.

One morning Mr Martin called Walter at his hotel- which had now given him a long-stay bargain rate: not much of a bargain in Walter's opinion, but when you're rich, it didn't matter too much. The old couple weren't interested in selling their property at that specific point in time, so he'd need to keep looking. He had another idea, though, and it was regarding another property- a larger one this time- which was owned by a lady who'd been widowed recently. He knew her and her family well. He felt that they might have some financial issues to do with the death, and other taxes. It was a sad state of affairs, but it might work out well for Walter, and indeed the lady and her family too, if she wanted to sell quickly and hoped to get a fair price for it. Her two eldest daughters had left the area for work but the youngest one had stayed: a daughter named Jo, who worked at the tourist office in Mougins.

"I know Jo," said Walter. "She's lovely. I met her a while ago. Should I speak with her directly? It won't affect the commission you'd earn."

"I'll tell you what," said Mr Martin. "Let me speak with Jo and her mother first. I've known the family for years. It'll make things easier."

"That makes sense," said Walter. "Of course, it would have been rude of me to confront her and enquire, especially at such a sad time. It must be the heat making me think like a madman."

Mr Martin told Walter not to worry, and then, saying their goodbyes, they both hung up.

Two days later, Walter walked up to the village for exercise with Vincent. He didn't have plans to drop in and see Jo. He knew that Mr. Martin would call when he had news; but as he passed the tourist office, Jo, who was sitting at her desk that faced out into the street, waved to him, and he waved back. It was late morning and there weren't many tourists around yet, so the office was quiet.

"Hello Walter," she said when he walked in.

"Hi."

"Hello Vincent," she said.

"How are you?" said Walter.

"I'm well, thank you. A little bored just now because no one is here, but I'm going to take my coffee break soon. Do you want to have coffee together?"

"Yes, that would be nice. I could do with one. Where shall we go?"

"Just across the road is good. We can sit in the shade."

Walter waited outside as Jo hung a "back in ten minutes sign" on the front door and then locked it. They walked across the road and sat outside under the shade, both ordering a coffee when the waiter appeared.

"Mr Martin spoke with my mother and me yesterday evening," Jo said.

"Ahhh. He didn't call me to tell me," said Walter. "But I've been out most of the morning. I'm very sorry if you were offended. It's just that Mr Martin said that he thought it might be a good idea if he were to talk with you and your mother."

"That's not a problem. I've known him all my life. He came to our house to speak with us last night and told us of your property searches, both of them. I have to be honest and say that Mr Martin's thoughts were interesting to my mother, me, and my two sisters. The property is far too big for me and my mother, and besides, I'm going to leave Mougins at some point soon with my boyfriend- we're going to Paris. Even if both my sisters had decided to move in with my mother the property would still be too expensive to run. So, we should talk."

She took a deep breath.

"If we were offered a good price, we would be interested, as long as…"

She took another deeper breath, and Walter wondered what was going to follow.

"…we knew exactly what you were going to do with the property, and the piece of land it sits on. You see, my family is from this village and it's important to us, and the mayor and the town council, to know what your plans would be."

Walter took all of this in and enjoyed the good strong coffee in front of him. What Jo said didn't put him off. It pleased him. He loved that she and the villagers cared about what went on in their village. It was a good sign.

"I'll tell you what," he said. "If you give me a day and time that suits, I'll come and visit you, have a look at the property, and tell you what I plan to do. I will be as honest with you as you are with me; if the property doesn't suit, I won't buy it. I have very specific things in mind, including a sea view or a mountain view. I don't know if..."

Jo cut him off.

"It has a sea view at the back and a view of the mountains at the front."

"A great start," said Walter.

They chatted for a while about the property and they both felt that there might just be an aligning of the stars. But until Walter had seen it, they wouldn't be sure. The chemistry between Walter and Jo was good though, and that helped because it built some trust and understanding. They finished their coffee, then Walter and Vincent walked back across the road with Jo, then waited while she called her mother.

"Tonight, come for dinner at eight- does that suit?" she asked him.

"Perfect."

Jo wrote down the address and handed it to Walter, saying, "Vincent is welcome too."

Chapter 35. Home. Mougins, August 1979

Walter slowly approached the property on his scooter just after eight, with Vincent sitting in front of him, and underneath the seat lay a bottle of Champagne keeping cool. He pushed the buzzer that was mounted on a pillar supporting one end of huge black, ornate, iron gates. He couldn't see inside the property at all, which was surrounded by a thin wire fence, barely visible, because it was covered in incredibly tall, multi-colored bushes that he'd later learn were called Rose Laurel; they were very common in the area.

A few seconds after pushing the buzzer, the gates swung inwards, allowing Walter to drive inside the property. Vincent had jumped off the scooter and ran ahead. What lay in front of Walter took his breath away. Sitting on perhaps two acres of land stood an old house which looked run down, but beautiful. It was nearer the back of the parcel of land which meant that there was perhaps a fifty- yard walk up to the house along a dirt path, and in front of it and at the sides of the house lay more land but with nothing on it.

The house looked tired, but it could easily be brought back to life. It comprised two floors and must have at the very least, three or four bedrooms Walter guessed. He could see from where he stood that the back of the house looked down to the sea, and the front where he now stood looked out over the hills. Built of old blonde stone, the house looked to be full of character. Tired, but stunning.

The front door opened, and Jo walked out to greet him, taking him by the arm and leading him inside to meet her mother. Vincent trotted behind them.

The inside of the house was clean, but also tired like the exterior. It had just as much going for it inside as the outside did though. To Walter, it felt like home the instant he stepped inside. It wasn't how it looked, but how it felt.

Jo's mother Anna, an elegant and beautiful woman in her sixties with blond hair and bright blue eyes came to meet him, and gave him a polite, but not warm smile. She was wary. Walter was taken through the living room at the front and out to the back garden, and from there, led to an old wooden table and chairs with cushions where they could sit, talk, and admire the view down to the deep blue sea. Walter wondered how he'd ever be able to properly negotiate a price for this property: the second he'd walked in he knew he wanted it, and that would make him a terrible negotiator.

Anna was wonderful. She'd obviously warmed to Walter very quickly for some reason, perhaps the same way that Walter had warmed to her and her house. She talked constantly, leaving him nothing to do other than listen and enjoy story after story about her life. Normally, someone who did this would be a bore; Anna was anything but.

After the three of them had finished the champagne that Walter had brought as well as the tasty dinner of rabbit stew eaten with great enthusiasm, Anna asked Walter to tell her about himself, and why he was possibly interested in buying the house and land. Walter took his time, expanding more than he'd usually do- because he had to- telling her where he was from, how he'd been fortunate to inherit well, and given that he wasn't enamoured with the country he was born in, he wished to create a new life for himself, there in Mougins. He talked about how he'd spent time in the army and then at chef school. Chef school really captured Anna's attention, and she asked probing questions about the course and what he'd learned. They were now on common ground, it appeared: food. Soon they were swapping story after story because Anna, like Walter, had attended the school in Paris, but never had any intention of being a chef.

"So, what do you plan to do for work then?" she asked.

"Open a café." And at that point Walter went on to explain about his plans for his café, the sparse menu- which both women loved- and the short opening hours.

"You could build the café in these grounds here, across from the house, nearer to the gates. It wouldn't block the view."

"Do you like the idea of a café, then?" asked Walter.

"I do, yes. But not if you simply plan to sell it in a couple of years."

"This would be my home. I don't think I'd ever go anywhere else."

"Come with me," said Anna, "Let me show you around the house then we can have a good walk around the grounds. I have an idea," she said, looking at Jo who smiled approvingly.

They went through every room in the house very slowly, with Anna talking about the history of the rooms, and what alterations had been done to them over the years. It turns out that her parents had built the house in the 1920s as a summer retreat. The grounds and the views were breath-taking, even in their current condition, and Walter could easily picture in his mind what he'd do to bring it all to life. He saw where he could build the café while keeping the home private from it, partially hidden from view by more Rose Laurel, plenty of olive trees and a cleverly sculpted garden. Even after doing that, there would still be plenty of land free. He could perhaps create another garden or grow his own vegetables. There were endless possibilities.

After the tour, they returned to the gardens at the back of the house which overlooked the sea and surrounding lands. The sea sparkled because the sun had set, and lights had been put on everywhere they looked, including the boats sitting in the calm water. The air smelled of the sea, the sand, flowers, palms. He was in heaven. Walter prayed the house and grounds would be affordable.

"How much do you think this place is worth, Walter?" asked Jo.

"Well, I love it, Jo. I'll be honest. But whether I'd make an offer or not would depend on whether I could get permission to build my café and run it in these grounds."

"That wouldn't be a problem, am I right?" said Anna to Jo.

"You are right," said Jo. She turned to Walter. "We know the mayor, the town council, everyone, and they know us," she explained.

"What's more," said Anna, "if you think my proposal makes sense, then you would never have any problems with bureaucracy, ever."

"And what's your proposal, Anna?"

"If you build me a small three-bedroom property on another plot of land which I own nearby, and which is much smaller than this one, and currently has nothing on it, then I would offer you this house and land at a competitive price. The piece of land I refer to is only perhaps the size of a tennis court- far too small for you."

"And how much would you sell me this house and land for?"

Anna turned to her daughter. "Jo, why don't you get the brandy out and we can talk further."

"A great idea," said Walter, smiling. Brandy solved so many awkward issues.

The three of them spoke until the wee hours. Each of them wanted to find a way to make this work, and eventually they agreed the parameters of a deal, but it was dependent on an evaluation of the house and land from Mr Martin, as well as an independent surveyor. They needed estimated building costs, with limits on them, not just for Walter's café but Anna's small home on her land. In Walter's mind, the biggest hurdle would be gaining official agreement from the mayor's office to build and run his café, despite Jo's assurances. It was surely going to be difficult.

The evening ended eventually, and feeling good, Walter headed off with Vincent. Anna had given Walter a rough indication of an asking price for her property and land, and it was only at that moment that Walter fully appreciated how rich he was. He could have paid for it ten times over.

Another meeting was set up for a week hence, which Mr Martin would be part of. By then Anna and Jo would have spoken to the mayor, and they would also have arranged a separate meeting with an architect friend of theirs, who could provide ballpark prices on the design and construction for the two buildings. The design for Anna's house already existed, and Walter could describe clearly enough his needs for the café to allow an architect to give a broad, estimated cost. It was all that was needed for Walter at this stage; just enough to ensure that there would be no unwelcome financial hurdles; but given the asking price of the house and land, he doubted that there would be. It would have been good business practice to bring in his own architect, but he decided against it, instead deciding that he'd invite Mrs Fox down to the meeting with Mr Martin and Anna's architect instead, after explaining who Mrs Fox was to Anna and Jo. They were both happy with that arrangement.

The week passed at speed. Mrs Fox, true to her word, came down and helped Walter. She was nothing short of brilliant. She and Anna got on like a house on fire and helped Walter when it came to fleshing out the details with the architect regarding the building of Anna's house and Walter's café. There would be no objections from the mayor or the town council according to Anna and Jo. Amazing. They took Walter to meet with the mayor in person, wearing a new shirt for the occasion, and the meeting went well, as predicted. The mayor was genuinely excited about Walter's café. He gave the project the thumbs up.

The only question that no one except Walter could answer, was what the café would be called.

"What are you going to call it?" asked Jo.

"I've got an idea in mind. I just need to think a little more before I finally decide. Can I tell you later?"

"Of course; it's your café Walter. You can do whatever you choose."

Chapter 36. Life. Mougins, November 1979.

Work started on construction of the café on the first day of November. The opening was planned for the following August, which would be ten years after Walter had walked into the army recruiting centre in Brighton. Given the limited size of the café, the building schedule was very manageable now that the design of it had been created and agreed upon according to Walter's brief.

Mrs Fox, Jo, Anna, the mayor– everyone– questioned Walter at least a couple of times about the menu and opening hours, because they couldn't understand how he would possibly make a profit with such limited opening hours and such a ridiculously tiny menu: croissants in the morning and Iberian ham and various cheeses (and olives) in the afternoon. That was it. The drinks menu was equally sparse. Coffee or tea, hot chocolate or water, or grapefruit juice in the morning. Bottled beer, wine, grapefruit juice or water in the afternoons and early evenings. And of course, only one cocktail on the menu: Mixed Elves. That was it.

Opening hours: 8am to 11am and a five-hour break before opening again at 4pm. It would then close at 8pm again. That was it. The plan baffled everyone, and the idea of only one cocktail, of which they'd never heard, simply left them stumped. Mrs Fox, who by this stage had returned to run her hotel and restaurant, was trying to help Walter with a business plan, but was becoming agitated during phone calls until he eventually told her that he didn't need to make a profit. He simply didn't want to lose money.

"Well why didn't you tell me that in the first place?" she said.

"I don't know- I should have. Sorry. I'm just so used to keeping things to myself. I'll improve. Promise."

"You'd better," she said, and hung up.

During the winter months, as the café was being built, Walter worked on the interior of his new home, having eventually managed to get Anna out of the house and into rented accommodation while her own new home was being built. Everything was moving along brilliantly because everyone was excited about what was happening. And everyone was happy. Good times.

Each morning, Walter would wake, then exercise, and then tackle whichever job he had to do as a matter of priority that day, whether it be painting walls in the house, or liaising with builders who were simultaneously renovating his home kitchen and bathrooms as well as building his café. It was full steam ahead. He had landscape gardeners working on his land, ensuring that there was a visual separation between his house and the café.

The landscape gardener had good ideas about how to use bougainvillea, helenium, mimosas, sunflowers, lavender, clematis, and olive trees which would make the front of the café stunning. The main entrance to the land where the gate stood would remain the same, but the paths to the house and the café would veer off in different directions just a few feet into the property. By the time the café opened, the house would be barely visible to anyone walking to the café. Parking would be outside.

On a cold evening close to Christmas, Walter decided to treat the entire building and landscaping team to dinner. Anna and Jo were also invited. He'd been pushing everyone hard, which sometimes didn't go down so well because they preferred to go at their own pace, and they saw schedules as rough guides as opposed to fixed timings that should be adhered to. For Walter, having spent six years in the army, and then a year in chef school, this attitude was very frustrating, and frequently he'd voice his opinions loudly and clearly which made him unpopular for a day or so.

Dinner, he decided, would be a nice thank you for the effort that was made, and would hopefully be a motivator for the team. They ate in a neighbouring village, and it was a rowdy night enjoyed by all. When everyone returned to work the next day, albeit late, Walter noticed a significant uplift in work rate among the team.

Christmas day arrived soon after, and Walter spent the day and evening alone with Vincent; the idea of accepting Anna's kind invitation to join her entire family for lunch was just too much. Instead, he made a roast leg of lamb for himself and Vincent which they both enjoyed. Walter hated rosemary and seemed to be the only person he knew who didn't like the herb with lamb, so his well-cooked roast was herb free. It was followed by a traditional sherry trifle which Vincent would have finished all on his own if Walter hadn't forced himself and the dog out for a long walk as darkness fell. As he walked, Walter thought about his life- past, present and future. Was he happy now? He wasn't sure what the answer was. He was certainly positive, and that was a step in the right direction.

Chapter 37. Prudence. Paris, August 1980

A long time had passed since Walter had left Paris to go south, and Prudence had arrived in Paris. Her work at Bar Pic– eighteen long and lonely months– was not something she enjoyed, and she planned to make a change. She'd met various people who she'd see socially sometimes but they hadn't become good friends. Paris wasn't a welcoming city, so she didn't really feel part of it.

Fate can be cruel sometimes. That night in April, the year before, just after she'd arrived, she and Walter had been standing less than fifty feet away from each other at Morocco restaurant: one of them inside and one outside. Walter had been inside, talking about Prudence and wondering where she was, and Prudence had been outside, thinking about Walter and wondering where he was.

Eighteen months later, having built up a little nest egg by living cheaply, Prudence decided to treat herself to dinner out one evening, and go to Morocco restaurant. She'd forgotten about its existence after she'd first laid eyes on it, but something had recently reminded her of it again– probably the smell of spices coming from one of the other restaurants she passed when leaving work each evening. And so, the following evening, her day off, she showered, dressed, and walked to Morocco restaurant, thinking of good food all the way there.

As she sat quietly alone at the very same table Walter had sat at when he visited, just as Walter had, she heard her name being called, and looked up to see Tarik.

"They should name this Reunion restaurant" he shouted.

"Tarik, what are you doing here?" She answered, very excited.

His was the first friendly face she'd seen in a long, long time.
He smiled at her, shaking his head.

"I can't believe it. I thought you were lost and gone forever. It is a miracle you're here. Actually, this should be called Miracle restaurant."

Prudence laughed.

"First Reunion then Miracle; both are good names for a restaurant, Tarik. Indeed, this is our reunion. Maybe not quite a miracle though. How have you been?"

Tariq responded, a serious look replacing the happy face.

"I called it "Reunion" because first I see Walter here and then I see you."

"You saw Walter. When?"

Prudence had the same serious look on her face now.

"Perhaps a year ago. More. But now he's gone. He told me he was leaving Paris and going to live in the sun. That's all he said. He didn't say where, exactly."

"He didn't say which city or town, just "the sun?""

"Yes."

Prudence put her hands to her face, then removed them and clapped loudly, causing other customers in the restaurant to look at her. At last, some good fortune. She knew Walter loved the sun. It was typical of him to keep his cards close to his chest and not say exactly where he was going. She felt it was most likely the south coast of France he'd gone to though, and not Spain where she'd just been.

"You must join me and my family for dinner. We must celebrate." Tarik said.

Unlike Walter, she accepted the generous invitation from Tarik, and spent the evening with him and his family, eating greedily, reminiscing, and drinking plenty, her mood lifted by good news, and good company.

Prudence assured Tarik that she had plenty of money. She needed no help, but she thanked him very much for the kind offer. Tarik could see her well-worn clothes and knew this not to be the case, but he didn't push. And once more, unlike Walter, Prudence agreed to keep in touch with Tarik when he produced a name card and handed it to her. He didn't ask her to name a date when they'd next meet, for he knew that very shortly, Prudence would be making her way south.

Chapter 38. Prudence. Lyon, August 1980.

Prudence rose from the hard, dark green wooden bench she was sleeping on in Park des Hauteurs, set high on a hill overlooking the city. It was sunrise, and despite it being the height of summer she was cold and tired. Benches were no place to sleep.

The light was beautiful though and she took a deep breath as she stretched, taking in the cool, fragrant air and the view of the city which were stunning, and stirred her senses, reviving her.

She'd been mugged on the train the evening before when it had stopped at Lyon station. Without a ticket and money or proof of identification, instead of being helped, she'd been told to get off the train.

She'd been asleep in an empty compartment when someone had come in and grabbed her rucksack which she was using as a pillow. When she groggily got to her feet she was punched on the head and fell to the floor. At knife point, she'd had to hand over the rucksack and luckily, instead of just running off with it, the mugger went through it taking her money, ticket and passport before throwing the rucksack back at her. He'd missed a little money stored in the secret compartment, but it wasn't enough to buy another ticket. Afterwards, shocked at the poor treatment she received from the conductor on the platform that she'd gone to for help, and still dazed, she'd made the unwise decision to continue her journey on foot and had walked in the wrong direction, ending up at Parc des Hauteurs late at night. Exhausted, she'd lain down on a park bench and fallen asleep.

The money in the secret compartment of her rucksack was enough for breakfast, so it looked like she was indeed going to have to walk hundreds of miles or more likely, walk the streets looking for another bar job to finance her onward train journey. She had immediate problems, too: nowhere to wash, nowhere to sleep and only enough money for breakfast but no lunch.

Cafés would be opening up– it was past dawn– so she wandered down the hill and out of the park.

Close to the entrance, resting against the front gate was a black bicycle, unattended. She looked around to see who the owner was but there was no one there. Had it been abandoned? Turning full circle she saw a park attendant- probably the first official of the day to start work at the park- standing up against a tree close to the park's entrance, relieving himself. Prudence wondered why he couldn't be bothered walking to one of the public toilets in the park. The answer to that, she assumed, was that he would think no one else would be nearby at such an early hour. Lazy. While the attendant was busy sorting himself out Prudence hopped onto the bicycle and set off for the southern coast, well over two hundred miles away. She'd beg, steal and permanently borrow, in order to get to where she wanted. She was a survivor.

Chapter 39. The Opening of Café Dawn, September 1980

In early July, Walter had created a list comprising people from his pre- Mougins life that he would consider inviting to the opening of his café the following month. He'd decided to be careful when it came to old army buddies in case there was talk of his money and where it had come from, or in fact, where he'd been. So, he didn't invite them. And he took the same precautions with Jacob, much as he would have loved to have him visit. There was just too much risk involved.

After going through an extensive list of people he'd known and been involved with over the past ten years, he ended up with a pre-Mougins guest list containing three names: Veronique, Vincent, and Mrs Fox. Three people. Well, it was better than none.

Anna, on the other hand, wished to invite just about everyone she knew, despite Walter saying that there was no need for her to do such a thing. He was happy with a quiet opening. They agreed that she'd only invite her closest friends.

As the opening neared, lots of people agreed to attend. The mayor had agreed to be there, as had the entire town council, and Jo, Mr Martin, Anna's forty closest friends, as well as several of Jo's friends too. The architect and all the builders and landscape gardeners would be there, along with Walter's new lawyers, accountants, and suppliers of kitchen equipment and produce.

Mrs Fox, who had come down a week early to help with the opening, showed Walter a list of over a hundred people. He nearly died. He knew he'd need to say a few words. The prospect tortured him.

Two days before the official opening, Mrs Fox had now taken almost complete control of events, including helping Walter hire the three members of staff she'd advised him he needed: a manager and two waiting staff, all from the village.

Walter stood outside of the now finished café, watching the sign being attached to the outside of the building. It was a burnished bronze sign in a low-key, soft rounded font, with an early morning sun resting snugly beside the name: Café Dawn.

Just as he'd done during his walk on Christmas evening, Walter thought about his previous life and everything he'd been through, right up until that morning in Paris when he'd sat astride his Vespa just after 6am, about to set off and build his new life in the sun.

From now on, for him- wee Walter Mack from Edinburgh- each dawn would mean life, opportunity and hope.

"It's a good name, Walter," said Anna who had joined him to watch, "It means "gift" in French."

"I know, but I'm going to think of the English word. It means more to me just now."

Opening day arrived and after the initial reluctance to mingle, Walter had a good time, despite worrying that he wouldn't. His café was alive with people enjoying themselves, and everyone was very complimentary about the design and the food that was on offer; the café's afternoon menu of Iberian ham, cheese and olives. It all went down a treat.

Walter took a seat on one of the vacant straight backed wooden chairs close to the entrance, watching and listening from a distance as a cellist played to the gathering. The notes and tones spoke volumes about the setting, the café, and the mood. They said everything about how Walter was feeling. He felt that the music did a better job of expressing his feelings at that moment than any speech he could ever give.

The time came for him to talk, and so he did, briefly, thanking everyone for coming, and for all the help he had getting to this day. As he looked out at the guests he paused and choked briefly as he saw kind and good people looking at him, wishing him well. They were all friends now. His words were warmly rewarded with applause, and at that point Walter wandered into the café and behind the bar to make himself a Mixed Elf.

The evening before, when Veronique arrived from Paris with Vincent, she had roared with laughter when introduced to Walter's dog. Vincent the chef was less impressed, especially the next day, as both he and the dog responded whenever the name Vincent was called.

But Vincent the chef took Walter aside after the opening speech and embraced him, telling him that he was proud of him- proud of the wonderful café he'd built, and proud to have him as a friend. Veronique joined them and hugged Walter too, asking if it was a tear she could see in his eye. Walter walked off.

The house was not yet complete but was well on the way, and even with rooms still being renovated was in a good enough state to accommodate Mrs Fox, Veronique, and Vincent the chef. Walter slept with Veronique and Vincent slept with Mrs Fox.

<u>Chapter 40. Walter Mack. September 1980.</u>

The smell of baking croissants inside Café Dawn made Walter's stomach rumble. He stood behind the counter looking at the customers who had already become regulars. They were perfect as far as he was concerned: friendly, not overly talkative, and polite; all local, with the occasional tourist and what Walter termed "foreign locals" who were people like himself- those from other countries who had set up home in the region.

What struck Walter as delightful and surprising was that many of his customers came both for breakfast and a late afternoon or dusk snack and drink on the same day, something he determined must be the mark of how well Café Dawn was doing what it was designed to do.

Despite the pre-opening concern some had voiced about the simplicity of his menu, it had been well received by those who came. The croissants were a hit. The Iberian ham was a hit. Everything was working according to plan.

An elderly lady named Catherine, with white/blonde hair who owned a collection of large wrist watches and had a ton of charm, had already claimed one of the indoor seats and tables as her own. Anyone sitting at her place, including Walter, had better be careful.

As the coffee brewed and mixed with the scent of croissants, Walter found a minute free and decided to sweep the café's stone floor. He didn't need to, but he enjoyed doing it. He could see the front door and the front terrace from where he stood, as well as the back door and the beautiful garden it led onto. The sun shone through the front and out to the back.

As always, he was a little tired, the usual break in sleep during the night meant he was never quite rested when he woke in the mornings. He'd had fewer nightmares which was positive, but they still came. He wondered if he'd ever sleep through the night.

Against everyone's advice, he had insisted that white linen napkins were always placed at each of the wooden tables. It created a lot of laundry but once again, Walter had been right. It seemed to work. It was old fashioned, but it brought a certain style and feeling of care and cleanliness to the café. Not snobbery. It was just nice. People liked nice things.

Walter knew that Catherine had stolen several napkins, but he didn't mind. He loved her.

He looked out to the lavender bushes growing around the terrace in the garden at the back and decided to go and water them when he'd finished sweeping. Like the sweeping, he didn't need to do it, but he wanted to. Patches of shade created by the parasols at the tables looked like tiny islands of respite from the strong southern sun.

There was a beeping sound from behind him meaning that the croissants baking in the oven were done. He'd have to continue sweeping later. One of his team, Luna, a young and beautiful hard-working woman born and brought up in Mougins was behind the counter serving customers who were waiting for his croissants. He put the broom in the store cupboard just off the kitchen at the back then went to the huge oven close to where Luna stood and removed a huge tray full of the very best croissants in the region.

Chapter 41. Mixed Elves. October 1980.

A skinny, sunburned, hungry young woman; a vagabond on a bicycle, rode towards Mougins. Her name was Prudence.

After leaving Lyon on her stolen bicycle, she'd worked her way down to the coast, making the odd small amount of money by washing dishes, working on building sites and sleeping rough. But she'd made it. And now, she was approaching the old village of Mougins, once more looking for work. She had hundreds of miles of coastline still to visit as part of her search, so once more she'd need to work, giving her time to ease up, eat better, sleep indoors perhaps, and plan her next move.

Earlier that day she'd washed on a beach under one of the public showers, and now, well-scrubbed, she felt she was in a presentable state to ask around for work.

She looked up at the old village high in the distance and thought it might be best to wait until it was a bit cooler before making the climb. She decided to look around the lower levels while she waited, so she set off, slowly pedaling the bicycle. A minute or so along the road she came to a wonderful looking place sitting at the end of a driveway, called Café Dawn. It looked to be closed, but there was a sign outside the front gates of the driveway saying, "Help Wanted."

The opening hours were 8am to 11am, and 4pm to 8pm only.

"How odd," she thought, wondering how on earth the place made any money. It was close to 4 pm, so she decided to sit in the shade outside the café, under a large parasol. She looked out to the mountains, admiring the breath-taking view. At 4pm, an old lady appeared from inside and approached Prudence who told her that she'd like to apply for the job, whatever it was. Anything was fine. The old lady led her inside, telling her that the owner would appear soon, and she should talk to him.

"Please wait here." she said.

Prudence took a seat at one of the tables and looked around, enjoying the cool air and the tranquility that the dimmed light and thick blonde stonework created. She picked up the food menu which was on a beautifully scribed card the size of a paperback novel. The menu was just as odd as the opening hours, and just as short.

A little past 4pm, the old lady returned to say that it looked like the owner was delayed, and passing Prudence a drinks menu, asked if she'd like something while she waited. Prudence thanked her, and the old lady stood patiently while Prudence read the menu. Prudence smiled to herself: it really was very funny. So short: wine, beer, water, grapefruit juice- and lastly, Mixed Elves.

She stared hard at the last item on the menu. A full minute went by, and she said nothing.

"Are you alright my dear?" asked the old lady, touching her cheek.

Without looking up, Prudence asked for a Mixed Elf but the old lady shook her head and apologised, telling her that only the owner knew how to make them.

Once again Prudence sat quietly, staring at the menu, saying nothing, not looking up.

"Are you sure you're alright?" asked the old lady.

"Is the owner's name Walter?"

"Yes, it is. Do you know him?"

The sound of a door opening at the back of the café stopped the conversation. A voice behind her asked:

"Where have you been?"

"Here and there; everywhere," she replied. "It's quite a story. I was looking for you."

She hadn't turned because she didn't want him to see her tears. She wiped them away.

Walter walked past her and sat so that they faced each other. They touched feet under the table, but said nothing because they didn't need to, instead being wholly content just looking at each other. The old lady rolled her eyes and walked away.

Prudence reached into her rucksack and took out the photograph of the two of them together at the café in Marrakech. And then digging into the rucksack again, and removing a pen, she scribbled over the photo then handed it to Walter. He read it. What was "my happiest day ever" now read: "my second happiest day ever."

"Yes." he said, "Today is the happiest."

Then they talked and talked and talked. At dusk, they drank beer and ate Iberian ham and cheese, interrupted only by friendly people stopping at their table to say hello.

Chapter 42. Sleepy head.

Prudence woke early. It was pleasantly dark in the room, and calm. She sat up, smiled, and swung round, putting her feet on the cool wooden floor. Tiny flecks of sunlight pierced through the wooden shutters. Turning, she gently shook the sleeping figure buried under the covers beside her. Walter had slept a deep, dreamless, and peaceful night.

Shaking him gently again she said, "Come on elf, time to get up. We have a café to run."

The End.

Acknowledgements:

Thank you to SLM, GM, CA, GM and DD for their time, help and their valuable thoughts. And to Georgia Nelson for her front cover design, and proofing.

Printed in Great Britain
by Amazon